NO MORE
TEARS IN THE
END

NO MORE TEARS IN THE END

ROY GLENN

www.urbanbooks.net

Urban Books
1199 Straight Path
West Babylon, NY 11704

ISBN- 13: 978-1-60162-162-7
ISBN- 10: 1-60162-162-0

First Printing June 2009
Printed in the United States of America

10 9 8 7 6 5 4 3 2 1

Distributed by Kensington Publishing Corp.
Submit Wholesale Orders to:
Kensington Publishing Corp.
C/O Penguin Group (USA) Inc.
Attention: Order Processing
405 Murray Hill Parkway
East Rutherford, NJ 07073-2316
Phone: 1-800-526-0275
Fax: 1-800-227-9604

NO MORE TEARS IN THE END

Chapter 1

Mike Black

"**B**ullshit, Mikey. You tellin' me that you whacked two DEA agents and you ain't worried?" Angelo Collette asked me after his seventh single malt scotch.

"Right."

"Get the fuck outta here. You're drunk."

"Right." Actually I was fucked up, so I said it. "I'm fucked up, but I ain't worried." And I wasn't.

Not really.

Near as I could tell the cops weren't up on me. And if my luck held up, and it hasn't been worth a shit lately, they wouldn't be.

Luck?

Fact was my luck with the DEA has been all bad. My wife Cassandra was brutally murdered; arranged by DEA agents, which is something else I don't understand. I've been out of the drug game for years.

My attitude about a lotta things changed after a very good friend, Vickie Payne, died smoking cocaine in my apartment.

My cocaine.

I've never done cocaine in my life, but back in the day I would always keep some around 'cause some women would freak for it. That night, André gave me some pure; just chipped it off the block, bagged it and handed it to me. When I got home the next morning, instead of puttin' a cut on it, I threw the bag on the coffee table and crashed on the couch.

I had been asleep a couple of hours I guess, when Vickie came in. We talked for a minute then I passed out again. When I woke up I decided to get in the bed, but the door to my room was locked. I knocked on the door, but Vickie didn't answer. After awhile I kicked the door in. I found her lying on the floor naked, with the pipe still in her hand. To me, cocaine is death and heroin is slow death. So I took steps to get out. Maybe it was time to get all the way out.

As Wanda has become very fond of tellin' me, we make just as much money from our legitimate businesses as we do from our other operations. Gambling, number running, loan sharking, and prostitution.

I've got no interest in the dope game at all. Don't get me wrong, I don't give a fuck how a muthafucka makes his money.

That's his business.

And as long as his business doesn't cut into mine, it's none of my business. It's all about business to me.

But this shit with the DEA ain't about business, it's personal. If you believe Bobby's version of it, it began years ago when I bitch slapped Diego Estabon. Back then, Diego was just Gomez Estabon's fresh off the boat, punk-ass kid, who was trying to make a name for himself in his daddy's drug business.

It was years later that Diego came up with some wild-ass scheme to implicate me in the game. Part of his plan involved kidnapping my wife Cassandra, and he died for it. I thought it would end there, but it didn't. That led to one of his partners, a DEA agent name Kenneth DeFrancisco, goin' to jail, and he blamed me for being there.

Me?

Why me?

Why not blame your dumb-ass partner for coming up with the dumb-ass plan?

Drunk or sober, I still haven't figured that out. But because he blamed me, DeFrancisco ordered Cassandra's murder. I killed him and everybody else that was involved in it. The only one left was another DEA agent named Pete Vinnelli, and I would get to him in due time. But these other two I never saw coming.

"Look, Angee, all I know is that these two fucks were plannin' to kill me. What the fuck was I supposed to do?" How the fuck was I supposed to know that they were DEA?

If I hadn't asked Jackie Washington, a very pretty robber-turned-gambler, who I've recently taken more of an interest in for more reasons than just business, to keep an eye on Mylo, I'd be dead now. Mylo used to run a high-stakes poker game for Freeze, but there was something about him that I didn't trust.

Not only did Jackie keep an eye on him; she set up surveillance on his ass. Had bugs in his office, had GPS trackin' on his ride and was tappin' his phone. That's one more reason why I don't like using those fuckin' things.

Phones I mean.

Jackie followed Mylo to a meeting with a man that I found out later was a DEA agent named Masters. She recorded the conversation and had pictures of the two of them at a meeting where they planned to kill me.

"So I killed them."

But the question still stood. How the fuck was I supposed to know that they were DEA?

The answer was simple.

I should have taken my time. After I got the information from Jackie, I should have checked them out. Found out why those fucks wanted me dead.

But I didn't.

As soon as I saw Masters sitting with Mylo at the fight I saw blood. I went after Masters, while Nick and Freeze took care of Mylo. That didn't work out so well either. Mylo shot Freeze and he died in Nick's arms.

I caught up with Masters at Meyers Garage on 34th Street. Once the parking attendant was out of the car, Masters jumped in and he rolled slowly toward the street. I stepped up to the car and fired three times. The first shot broke the glass. The next two hit Masters in the head.

"I ain't sayin' that you was wrong, Mikey," Angelo said. "If it was me, and I'm glad it ain't."

"Thanks." I interjected.

"No problem. If it was me, and they were comin' at me like they was comin' at you, I'da whacked them too. That's all I'm sayin'."

"I'm glad you see it my way," I said and downed my seventh glass of Remy. No way I was lettin' Angee out drink me. "All I'm sayin' is that they're dead, and I'm here gettin' drunk with you."

Chapter 2

I'd known Angelo Collette since we were in high school. We were both on the same path, but traveling in different directions. He became a soldier for Vincenzo Adalberto. Now he's got his own crew. I went to work for André Hammond. Back then, André controlled most of the illegal activity uptown and I was his enforcer.

When I was fifteen, me and my best friend Bobby Ray started out sellin' weed and doing a little number runnin'. But André was a drug dealer. As far as he was concerned, gambling and prostitution were just sidelines. That all changed when André was murdered. I took over his gambling operations and got out of the drug business.

"All I'm sayin' is that whackin' DEA agents is bad business. But you gotta handle shit the way you handle shit. You killed them."

"Haven't you heard? I'm a killer."

"I fuckin' know that. I was there when you made your bones, Mikey," Angelo said.

"No you weren't. You were there for number two. I

was there when you made your bones, Angee. Nickie Nemecek. Two shots: One to the chest; one to the dome."

"Make sure he's gone," Angelo said and raised his glass. "And I was too there when you made your bones."

"No, Angee, I couldn't do it 'cause of the kid. Remember?"

Angelo took another swallow and I guess he thought about it. "You know what? You're right. His little girl came out the house and you backed off."

"I knew you'd remember."

"You did the right thing. I couldn'ta shot him in front of his kid either."

"What did you say?"

"What, are you drunk? I said you fuckin' did the right thing. Shootin' him in front of his kid wouldn'ta been right."

I got up and punched Angee in the face. He fell off his chair and hit the floor hard.

"What the fuck, Mikey!"

I helped him get up then sat down, and poured us both another drink.

"What the fuck you hit me for?" Angelo asked and shot his drink.

"You woulda done the same shit?" I shot mine and poured us another.

"Yeah. Whackin' the guy in front of his family ain't right."

"Now it ain't right. Now it ain't fuckin' right! Is that what you're sayin', Angee? The shit ain't fuckin' right! After all these fuckin' years later, and now you say it ain't right."

"Yeah, that's what I'm sayin'. What the fuck is wrong with you?"

"Back then it was all about how I was a chicken shit, a punk, that I was a fuckin' coward!"

"I never said that shit."

"Yes, you fuckin' did, Angee. The whole way back to André's that's all you kept sayin'. Chicken shit!"

Angee took another sip of his drink, and started nodding his head. I guess he remembered that too. "I guess you're right. I did say that shit."

"You know how long I carried that shit around?" I respected Angee; wanted him to respect me. I didn't want him thinkin' I was a coward.

"Sorry, Mikey. I didn't know that shit bothered you. You wanna lay down on the couch and tell me about it?"

"I'm 'bout to take out my gun and shoot your ass."

"If that's what you're gonna do to make it right, Mikey, go ahead and shoot. But you'll miss me." Angee finished his drink and motioned for me to drink up so he could pour me another. "So you gonna tell me about it?"

"About what?"

"Your first."

"First what?"

"What the fuck have we been talkin' about? How you made your bones!" Angee said, much louder than I needed him to.

"Why you yellin'?"

"I'm not yellin'." Angelo poured me another drink.

I took a swallow. "When I got back to André's, he was there with Bobby and five women."

"Five of them?

"André was the king of the orgy, and he didn't mind sharin'. After the women left I told him what happened, and after they both had a good laugh, he told me and Bobby to go a little bar up on Bronxwood later that night," I said and laughed.

"What's so funny?"

"That bar is a church now."

"Go figure."

"Anyway, he gives us a picture of these two guys, and

tells us what he wants us to do. Since I'd just got punked out on a job, he asks me if I'm sure I can handle it."

"Hell yeah, I can handle it," I told André that day. I was pretty sure that none of their kids would be hangin' out with them at the bar. "The rest of the day, neither me or Bobby did much talkin'," I continued tellin' Angee, "which was rare for Bobby. Truth was, we were both nervous, especially since I had just fucked around and couldn't kill Chicago."

Angee's facial expression changed. He put down his glass and looked at me. "You know, until you said his name, I forgot who he was and what that meant to you."

"You are drunk." Chicago was Cassandra's father, and it was Angee who put me on to it 'cause I had no idea that they were related.

"I know that shit, Mikey."

"You wanna hear this shit or not?"

Angee raised his glass. "Go ahead."

"When we get to the spot, the guy won't let us in."

"Why not?"

"He said we looked too young to be in there, until Bobby said that André sent us. After that it was all good."

Once we went in and sat down I asked Bobby, "What you tell him that for?"

"It got us in, right?" Bobby said. "And besides, André wants everybody to know it was him behind it."

I couldn't argue with his logic.

"Just relax. Have a drink and enjoy yourself," Bobby said and stared at the lone naked dancer behind the bar. "You ain't scared are you?"

"No! And don't you start with me. I heard enough of that shit from Angelo."

"Angelo." Bobby shook his head. "Why you hangout with that guy anyway?" Bobby tolerates my friendship with Angee, but he never did like him, and wonders why I do.

"Angelo's a good guy. Give him a chance. He's gonna be a good guy to know," I told Bobby that night and we waited.

It was two in the morning before the guys we were looking for got there. I tapped Bobby on the shoulder.

"You ready?" I asked and Bobby nodded.

We both put on gloves and stood up.

"Let's do it," Bobby said, and we walked toward them at the bar.

Once we were standing behind them, it was like time was standing still. I can't speak for Bobby, and we never talked about it after it was done, but honestly, its one thing to talk shit about doin' it, but pullin' the trigger and blowin' a hole in the back of somebody's head is another. To that point, we had collected money and roughed up a few people, which was fun, but we were about to kill these muthafuckas.

We never even knew their names, much less who they were and what they had done for André to want them dead. But the time for thinkin' was past; nothing to do then but pull and blast. I looked at Bobby, we pulled out our guns and we fired.

"What happened then?"

"What do you think happened? We dropped our gats and got the fuck outta there."

"What you gonna do now?" Angee asked after another swallow.

"I'm gonna kill the corner of this Remy and get outta here." I picked up the bottle and poured the last of the Remy into my glass, and maybe for the first time, was glad that Bobby made me get a driver.

He said that with all that we had goin' on lately—

muthafuckas tryin' to kill me and shit—that I needed to have somebody with me at all times and he couldn't always be there.

At first I resisted it. I don't need no fuckin' bodyguard. But I knew he was right, so I got a driver.

His name is Kevon. He used to work for Jamaica in the Bahamas. He drove me around on my last trip. I picked him because he didn't know anybody in this country, so his loyalty to me and only me wouldn't be a question.

"I'm talkin' about this other DEA fuck. What's his name?"

"Vinnelli."

"What you gonna do about him?"

"What you think I'm gonna do? I'm gonna kill him."

"You sure that's the best idea right now?"

"What do you mean? This is the muthafucka that arranged Cassandra's murder. He gotta die." I drained my glass and stood up. I was a little shaky, but I kept my balance.

"Where you goin', Mikey? Sit down and have another drink."

"I'm out, Angee."

"Well sit down anyway and think about this."

I sat down and Angee poured scotch in my glass. "Think about what?"

"You shouldn't push your luck. You got away with killin' those other two assholes 'cause they couldn't tie them to you, but Vinnelli, that might not go away that easy."

I started to argue with him but was too buzzed, and besides, I knew he was right.

"All I'm sayin' is that just 'cause you don't see them, don't mean they ain't coming."

"You right about that."

"If you want my advice—and I notice that you ain't

NO MORE TEARS IN THE END   11

askin'—but if you want my advice—you'll back off this thing and go back to doin' business."

"You're right, Angee."

"I know I'm right. So you gonna back off this shit, right, Mikey?"

"I'll leave it alone, Angee." I wasn't sure if I meant it or if I was just tellin' him that shit.

"And I got your word on this? You're gonna leave that shit alone and get back to business."

"You have my word." But now I had given my word.

Chapter 3

Nick

"That's it, Nick. That's it, baby. Fuck this pussy, Nick!" Wanda yelled as I took her from behind.

Under that business-like appearance and that cool, calculating demeanor, Wanda was *all* woman.

Wanda and I had been friends since we were kids. She was the first person that I met when I was sent to live with my grandmother after my parents disappeared. I guess you could say that our *relationship* began when I was a suspect in four drug-related murders.

Since that night the two of us began spending time together, you know; just two friends that like to hang out together. But we were feelin' each other. We finally got together while Black was in jail, accused of his wife's murder. Not exactly the best of circumstances for us to get together, but it is what it is.

Being the private person that she is, Wanda insisted that we keep our relationship on the low. She didn't want anybody to know about it; especially Mike Black, but I ended up telling him about it anyway. I thought that it was better coming from me.

I held her hips in place and pushed myself deeper inside her, but my mind wasn't on Wanda, sex, or anything close to it.

There was a song by The O'Jays back in the day that went something like: *Your body's here with me, but your mind is on the other side of town.*

Well that's exactly what and how I was feeling, and it wasn't 'cause of some other woman on the other side of town that I was messin' around with.

My mind was on 35th Street in Manhattan. In my mind's eye, one of my closest friends is dying in my arms and there is nothing I can do to help him.

This nightmare began the night Frank Sparrow defended his middleweight crown at The Garden. When I got there with Wanda, Black said he wanted to talk to me. Both Wanda and I cringed, thinking that he had found out about our covert relationship and was about to make good on his threat to kill whoever it was that Wanda was involved with. But what he wanted was something that I never expected to hear from him. "I need you to watch Freeze."

"Freeze? Why?"

"His boy Mylo arranged for Frank to take a dive."

"What?"

"Told Frank I wanted him to do it."

"You think Freeze knew about it?"

"I don't think so, but this nigga Mylo is his boy. Keep your eye on Freeze, but you don't let Mylo outta your sight."

"I'm on them, Black."

That was the promise that I made.

And the promise that I didn't keep.

After the fight, Sparrow jumped up on the ring ropes and pointed his glove at Mylo. Black hadn't counted on Sparrow calling Mylo out like that. We had to fight our way through the crowd to catch up with him. As soon as Mylo and Masters could, they separated.

"Freeze, you and Nick get Mylo. Bring him to the parlor. I'll meet you there." Black told me that night.

"Where you goin'?"

"Get Mylo."

"What about him?" I asked quietly since he thought Freeze might have been involved in the plot.

"He's good. Just get Mylo," Black said, and he and Bobby went after Masters.

All they knew was that Masters was involved with Mylo in the plot to kill Black, and that was enough reason to kill him. They both turned out to be DEA.

By the time we caught up with Mylo he had made it out of The Garden and was on 35th Street. He was startled when me and Freeze caught up with him in the crowd. "Where you goin' in such a hurry?" Freeze asked as soon as he was close enough to put his hands on him.

"Nowhere. Just tryin' to get out of here. You know, get back to the house; see how things are goin'."

"You not goin' to the after party?" Freeze asked as we walked alongside of him through the crowd.

"Yeah, I'ma stop by there later; you know, once the real after party gets goin'."

"You oughta come ride with us," Freeze told him.

I guess Mylo knew that if he went anywhere with us that we would kill him the first chance we got, and he was right. Mylo reached for his gun and turned to Freeze.

He fired two shots.

Freeze grabbed his stomach and fell into my arms. I laid Freeze on the ground. "Don't let him get away, Nick," Freeze told me as he grimaced through the pain.

I looked around and didn't see Mylo anywhere. He was gone. "I'm not leaving you." I said and held onto Freeze.

How could I have been so stupid?

Why didn't I take Mylo's gun right away?

It's my fault that Freeze is dead. Even though they tell me that it's not, I know better. Freeze is dead 'cause I got careless. And even though I avenged his death so Freeze could rest in peace, I haven't found any peace for myself.

Freeze started workin' for Black when he was sixteen years old. He was a kid, but Black saw something in him. That's what we used to call him, the kid. Back then, all Freeze did was run little errands for Black and hang out at the club messing with the ladies. That all changed one night after we robbed a warehouse and somebody robbed our load.

The next night when I got to The Late Night, Freeze was there talkin' to Black. They sat there for most of the night, and then Freeze jumped up and headed for the door. A couple of days later, Freeze had caught all of the guys that robbed us.

After that, Black made me work with Freeze. I had mad respect for the kid for catching them muthafuckas by himself. But he was just a kid; I didn't wanna work with him. The way shit worked was, since Black doesn't like to drive, whenever he had a little job to do, he would call me and say "come scoop me up."

Only this time when I get there, Black is nowhere to be found and Freeze gets in the car. "Let's go."

"Go where? Where's Black?"

"Black wants me to go with you."

"Why?"

"He didn't say why. He just said when Nick gets here that I should go with you."

I put the car in drive and pulled off. "Where to?"

"Spot off Boston Road."

"Who we goin' to see?"

"You know Harry Walker, right?" Freeze asked as I drove.

"Greasy?"

Yeah, I know his fat ass. He was a gambler who liked to bet on football, but Greasy had a string of bad luck. Lost a lot of money one Sunday then tried to bet his way out of it; as some gamblers are known to do. Now he owed one of our bookies a hundred grand.

We waited outside Greasy's apartment building, waiting for him to come home for the night. Neither of us had much to say while we were waiting, just listened to the radio, and watched the door. I was thinkin' about whether it was good idea for Black to send Freeze along with me. I didn't think he was up to it.

It was after three in the morning when Greasy got to his apartment. He was in the company of a very pretty full-figured woman.

As soon as Freeze saw Greasy headed for the building, he was out the car. I gave him points for enthusiasm. I was anxious to see if he got any points for style and more importantly, effectiveness.

By the time Greasy wobbled to the door and got his keys out, Freeze was on him. He put his gun to the back of Greasy's head. "What the fuck!" I heard Greasy say when I finally got to the door.

"Unlock the door and go inside," Freeze ordered the big man.

"What the fuck is goin' on?"

"Black sent me."

"Who the fuck are you?"

"I'm the nigga that's gonna shoot you and the titty bitch here if you don't unlock the fuckin' door."

Greasy unlocked the door and we went inside. Freeze told the woman to sit down and be quiet, while he backed Greasy up to the wall at gunpoint. It was only then that Greasy recognized me. "Nick? That you, Nick?"

"What's up, Greasy?" I said and took a seat next to his big tittie companion.

And they were pretty titties too.

I put my gun on my lap and she smiled at me. She looked like the sight of my gun and all that was going on was exciting her. Maybe she was just hoping that those big-ass titties would allow her to walk out with her life. Truth was she had nothing to worry about. At least I didn't think so. Freeze never said if Black wanted them dead or not, but I knew Black didn't like killing women.

"Who the fuck is this kid, Nick?" Greasy asked and Freeze punched him in his stomach for asking. He doubled over in pain.

"I already told you who I am," Freeze said calmly. "I'm the nigga who's gonna put a bullet in your head if you don't do what I tell you, which means you don't talk unless I tell you to." Freeze hit him in the stomach again. "Understand?" And then he hit him in the stomach again. This time Greasy went down to one knee. Those shots to the gut had taken all the wind out of him.

"Okay, okay," Greasy said, sucking air, trying to catch his breath.

At that point I knew Greasy wasn't gonna be any trouble, at least not that night. I was impressed with the way Freeze had taken control of the situation, just like Black would have.

What I didn't know, and didn't find out until much later, was that Freeze had been rollin' with Black. Freeze had learned his craft directly from Mike Black. Like I said, Black doesn't like to drive, and at the time, Freeze didn't know how to drive, so they would take the train. Picture that; they do what they gotta do, and then walk calmly back to the train station and go back uptown.

It only took a few more shots to the gut before Greasy went on and handed Freeze twenty large, and promised to have the rest in three days. "Three days, big boy, no more," Freeze threatened and we left.

After that night, Freeze and I got tight, as close as brothers. He saved my life and I saved his. When I was accused of murder and needed somebody to ride with me to settle things, Freeze was right there. Ride or die, just like it always had been, even though he hadn't seen me in ten years. Now he was gone and it was my fault; my fault because I was careless.

Chapter 4

I looked over at Wanda. She had curled into the fetal position and had drifted off to sleep. I guess she woke up when I got out of bed and walked to the window.

"You all right?" Wanda asked and sat up in the bed.

"I'm good," I said without looking back at her.

"You sure?"

"Yeah, I'm fine."

Wanda got out of the bed, wrapped the sheet around her body, and joined me at the window. She put her arms around my waist and I put my arm around her.

"Don't get me wrong. I'm not complaining, really I'm not. But you weren't there a while ago."

"I'm sorry." And I was. "I'll do better next time." And I will.

"It's not that it wasn't good. Lord knows it was. It just would have been better if you were in it with me."

"I thought I was all up in it."

"You know what I mean."

"I know."

"You gotta let it go, baby."

"I know."

"You want me to call around, find somebody for you to talk to about it?"

"What do you mean, like a shrink?"

"Yes."

"No. I ain't crazy. And I don't need no fuckin' shrink," I said louder than I needed to and felt bad after I said it.

Wanda let me go and walked away. She went in the bathroom and slammed the door. Even though I didn't really want to, I went in after her. She had turned on the water and was about to take a shower.

"Look, Wanda, I'm sorry. I didn't mean to snap at you. I know you're just trying to help."

Wanda turned around quickly. "Then let me help you, Nick, please. Talk to me. Don't shut me out like this. Let me in. Tell me what you're feeling. I know you're mad, I know you're hurting. It might make you feel better if you let it out instead of keeping all that rage bottled up inside you."

"I just need something to do; something to occupy my time and my mind."

Freeze dying changed a lot of things. Black was back, set up at Cuisine, the supper club he opened years ago, and he's running things from there. He had been staying out in Rockland County with Bobby. He moved out there after his wife, Pam, had a nervous breakdown. Now he was back running Impressions, the dance club that I had been running. That left me with nothing to do.

Black told me that I could do anything I wanted to in either side of the business. Naturally Wanda, who didn't like me working at the club, wanted me to think about doing something on the legit side of the house, but I ain't really feeling any of that shit. She's been talking up me taking over the finance company. All of it seemed like major boring shit.

"Have you given any more thought to what you might want to do?"

"I been thinkin' about some things."

"Like what?"

"Well," I replied and paused. "I been thinkin' seriously about talkin' to Black about me taking over the game."

"The game?"

"Yeah, the game," I said and walked out of the bathroom, 'cause I knew what was coming next, and I really wasn't in the mood to hear it.

The game I was referring to was a high-stakes poker game that Black and Bobby used to run back in the day. After Black got married and moved to the islands with Shy, a few people ran it until Freeze put Mylo in charge of it. Since I killed Mylo, the game was now being run by Jackie Washington, but she's in over her head.

As expected, Wanda turned off the water and came out after me. Like I said, Wanda wants me to do something on the legit side. She had a real problem with me running the club. Two problems actually. One was it kept me out all night, and with her working during the day we didn't see much of each other. Her solution to that was to hang-out at the club all night with me, which brings me to the other reason. Wanda was extremely jealous, very possessive, and just a bit insecure. Me taking over the game would just mean more of the same for her.

"Why?" Wanda asked. "Why the game?"

"That game is important to Black, and you and I both know that Jackie can't handle it."

Knowing I was right about Jackie, Wanda sucked her teeth and sat down next to me on the bed. "I don't know what he was thinking when he put her in charge of that game. Too much money passes through that game for her to be there and can't handle it."

"That's why I think it would be a good spot for me."

"Yeah, I know. And you're right. But we talked about this, Nick, and I thought we decided that you were going to look at doing something on the legitimate side of the house? I was under the impression that you were leaning toward taking over the finance company or running the real estate office."

"I know we talked about it, but I know how I am and I would be bored to death doing a desk job."

"I would make all that better for you as soon as you got home from work."

I put my arm around her and kissed her on the cheek. "I know you would, but I gotta do what's right for me."

"What about us?"

I wanted to say something like "what about us?"

"What about doing what's right for us, Nick?"

"You're right, Wanda, but I gotta be right with myself or there is no us." I guess that wasn't the right answer 'cause Wanda got up and hit the shower.

Oh, well.

It is what it is.

Chapter 5

Nick and Wanda arrived at Crave on 42nd, a restaurant located, as the name suggests, on 42nd Street, between 11th and 12th Avenue, waiting for Black and Bobby to arrive. While they waited, the pair munched on Prince Edward mussels in white wine and garlic sauce, and tried not to talk about the two things that Nick didn't want to talk about: The death of Freeze and what he was going to do now.

That's what Wanda wanted to talk about. But their meeting with Black and Bobby was about what to do now that Freeze was dead, and she was sure that the discussion would inevitably lead to a discussion about Nick's future, so Wanda decided to hold her tongue.

When Bobby announced that he was coming back to run Impressions, nobody was happier to hear that than Wanda. Relieved was more the word for how she felt about it. *Now maybe I can get a good night's sleep,* Wanda thought when she heard the news. While Nick was running the club, Wanda would be there every night. Most nights she would be there until the club closed. Then she would get a couple of hours of sleep and go to work.

The fact was Wanda was a jealous woman. The sight or even the idea of a woman, *any woman,* getting too close to Nick seemed to drive her mad. She had always prided herself on not being one of "those" women who were so insecure that they couldn't stand for their man to be out of their sight, but there she was, one of "those" women, and it bothered her. It just didn't bother her enough to keep her home at nights when he was working. She fell asleep many a night on the couch in Nick's office.

Wanda thought back to one night at the club when they talked about it. She remembered Nick shaking his head and saying, "The point is that you don't trust me."

"It's not that I don't trust you," she lied as she got up from the couch. She walked over to the window in the office that overlooked the dance floor and pointed. "It's those half-naked bitches down there that I don't trust."

"Why? I don't want any of them. Wanda, I love you."

"I know that, Nick, but I just don't understand for the life of me why you have to chat up every half-naked tramp in the club."

Wanda knew it wouldn't be like that if Nick took over the game. Other than a few working girls, and the occasional poker player, there wouldn't be many women to throw themselves at him. Her only issue was that if he took over the game, he would still be out at night. That meant that she would still never see him unless she posted up there every night.

It was a quarter past nine when the hostess escorted Bobby to the table. "Thank you, honey," Bobby said and handed the attractive hostess a twenty. "And if you don't mind, beautiful, would you send our waiter, please," he said as he sat down.

"I would be happy to," the woman said and slipped the bill in her pocket.

"You're very pretty," Bobby said watching the hostess as she turned and walked away.

Wanda shook her head. "Aren't you still married?"

"Pam and I have an understanding," Bobby said and continued to watch the hostess. She waved to him when she turned and noticed that he was watching her.

"What understanding is that?"

"She understands that if she isn't gonna give me any pussy that somebody is," Bobby said and continued to flirt with the hostess.

"Whatever. You still don't have to be all out in the open with it."

"What's the matter; you afraid that I'm a bad influence on Nick?"

Wanda looked Bobby in the eye. "Yes."

"Nick is a grown man."

"Excuse me," Nick interrupted. "Nick is sitting right here and can speak for himself.

"I'm sorry. I shouldn't have said that," Wanda said. But she meant what she said. "I just liked you better when you didn't cheat on your wife."

At one point, Bobby was a devoted married man and a good father to his four children. That changed when he met a dancer named Cat. It began shortly after Black left for the Bahamas with Cassandra and Freeze had taken over running the organization. Wanda thought that Freeze was running the organization into the ground and told Bobby that he needed to be more active in the business. He met Cat one night while he was at Cynt's.

She was dressed in a black cat suit with a small tail and mask to match. Bobby watched her as she approached somebody at the bar and started talking. "Who is that?" Bobby asked Freeze that night.

"That's Cat. She just started workin' here a couple of weeks ago. Cynt says words can't describe the way she dances. Said it's something you just have to experience."

"I'd be interested to see," Bobby said.

"I can arrange that," Freeze said. "Yo, Cat!"

Cat excused herself from the person she was talking to and came to see what Freeze wanted. "What's up, Freeze?"

"Cat, I want you to meet somebody. This is—"

"Bobby Ray," Cat said as she stepped closer to Bobby. "I've been wantin' to meet you for a long time."

"Really? And why is that?" Bobby asked.

"Because powerful men turn me on," Cat said and grabbed his hand. Freeze laughed as he watched Cat lead Bobby upstairs to the private rooms.

That's how it began and it went on until Cat started monopolizing more of Bobby's time and began calling Pam to boast about it. Another woman calling the house talkin' shit to her about her husband was absolutely unacceptable to Pam, and she was forced to take steps to put an end to the affair. Ultimately, her solution caused Pam to have a nervous breakdown.

Bobby got help for her and checked her into a private clinic and then moved his children to a house close to the clinic so Pam could see their children everyday while she recovered. When Pam came home she was feeling like herself again, but she refused to have sex with Bobby.

"I thought that since she was feeling better, and since the two of you seemed to have moved past all that stuff, that you and her were—" Wanda said.

"I thought she would too, but she said she can't. She said that she understands that I'm a man and I have *needs*," Bobby laughed. "Just show her respect and keep it away from her and the kids." Bobby picked up the menu.

"Well, if you don't mind, put me on that list of people you keep it away from."

Bobby turned to Nick. "Where's Mike?"

"I thought he was coming with you?"

"Ain't no tellin' what time he's gonna get here then," Wanda added. "Why he has somebody driving for him that don't know where anything is, is still a mystery to me."

"We're on 42nd Street. How hard could this place be to find?" Nick asked.

"Kevon used to drive him around in the Bahamas and Mike trusts him. That's good enough for me," Bobby said.

"It oughta be, since it was your bright idea for him to have a driver," Wanda said.

"Only question is, how long we gonna wait for him?" Nick asked. "I'm hungry."

"You're always hungry," Bobby said as their waiter arrived at the table.

"Are you ready to order?"

"We're still waiting on one more person," Wanda informed the waiter.

"Bring me a Remy Martin on the rocks," Bobby ordered.

"I'll have another Johnny Black," Nick added. "I think we should go on and order."

"Go ahead. I'll order something for Mike," Wanda said.

Bobby put down his menu. "What do you recommend?"

"I highly recommend the saffron-spiked lobster ravioli. The signature black truffle mac and cheese was served on season one of Bravo's 'Top Chef.' It's a tasty blend of black truffles; brandy and fontina slow-cooked with fresh thyme and oregano. The oversized scallops are doused in a buttery pool of vanilla bean cream. And our roasted salmon is served with a sweet sherry brandy glaze. All of those are excellent."

The trio gave the waiter their orders and he left them. They talked about the business at hand while they waited for Black to get there. He arrived at the table just as the food was being served.

"Sorry I'm late. We had a run to make, and on the way here Kevon went the wrong way on the Major Deegan and then we got stuck in traffic on the Cross Bronx," Black said and sat down. "Did you order me something?"

"I got you the smokey-rubbed filet mignon," Wanda replied as the server placed a plate of veggie pasta in front of her. Nick had the Chilean sea bass, while Bobby opted for the hoisin & cider pork tenderloin.

"What's that you havin'?" Black asked Wanda.

"Veggie pasta."

"You shoulda got me that, but this is cool."

While they enjoyed their meal, Wanda went over the state of their business. First she went over the legitimate business, telling her partners how strong profits were and gave a very optimistic outlook for the future. However, when she went into the state of their gambling operations, the report was not as good.

"So what you're sayin' is money is down across the board?" Bobby asked.

"That's exactly what I'm saying," Wanda said and took a sip of her drink.

"What are you really sayin', Wanda?" Black asked.

"What do you mean?"

"Stop it, Wanda," Bobby said. "You know exactly what he's askin' you. If you been in his ear, like you been in mine, all I can say is I feel sorry for you, Nick."

Wanda looked around the table, and slowly the corners of her lips curled into a smile. "What?" her smile turned to laughter.

"Go ahead and say it, Wanda. You think we need to get out," Black said without looking at her while he cut his filet. "I mean, that is why you got us all together to tell us the same shit you've been tellin' all of us individually for months. Or did you just want to go out to dinner?"

"He's right." Nick turned to Wanda. "You have been beatin' us all over the head with that club."

"Traitor. I'll deal with you later," Wanda whispered to Nick. "Yes, I think we should consider it seriously. Or at least we all could discuss it."

"Okay, counselor." Black put down his fork and knife. "Since you already made the point that we're making more money on the legit side of the house, go ahead and make your case."

"For one thing, we used to need a bigger table to have these meetings."

No one said a word.

No one had to.

Since she had everyone's attention, Wanda continued to drive her point. She reached out and held Black's hand. "It seems like we're moving backwards instead of forward. I mean look at the two of you. Mike, you had left all this behind you. You and Cassandra made a life for yourselves in the Bahamas. You were out. Then you let her talk you into staying here. You lost your wife and Michelle lost her mother. Which one of you is gonna be next? I'll be honest; I don't want to go to anymore funerals for a long time. I don't want to lose anymore friends. And the fact is we don't have to live like that anymore.

"And Bobby, while Mike was gone, you were so busy being a faithful husband and a father to your children that I had to practically drag you out of the house."

"True that," Bobby had to admit.

"And look what happened when you did get out," Wanda added.

"You had to go and throw that in."

"Well, it's the truth. And now Freeze is dead. Hasn't this life cost us enough?"

Black looked at Wanda for awhile without speaking. She was right, as usual. Actually, he had been thinking the same thing lately. It was as if life had come full circle for him. He was back in New York, back running Cuisine. He was seeing a stripper or former stripper at this point, along with a few others. Everything was like it was before he met Cassandra.

He thought about Michelle.

"All right, now that you've killed my appetite, I have two questions," Black said.

"What's that?" Wanda asked.

"Since we are still making money on gambling and our other businesses, if you do get out, how do you plan on replacing that income?"

Now it was Wanda who was looking at Black without speaking. She hadn't expected him to ask that, so she didn't have an answer ready. "I haven't given that any thought," she was forced to admit.

"What's the second question?" Nick asked.

"How do we get out? I mean what do we do, just walk away from it all? Do we make everybody buy us out?"

"I hadn't thought of that either," Wanda admitted quickly. Now her appetite was gone.

"When you have an answer to both of those questions, we'll talk about this again."

"Yes, sir," said a defeated Wanda. She had taken her shot, but she wasn't prepared. That wouldn't happen again.

"Don't get me wrong. Everything you said is true. I've been thinking about gettin' out before Michelle loses her father too. Maybe it's time."

"What about Vinnelli?" Nick wanted to know.

"I gave Angelo my word that I'd let that go."

"Angelo?" Bobby questioned. *Now that Angelo thinks it's a good idea he gives his word,* he thought. Bobby had been saying all along that after what happened with Masters and Mylo that Black should back off of Vinnelli.

"Well for once I agree with him," Wanda said. "We dodged a bullet with Mylo and that other character, no point pushing our luck any further."

Bobby got up from the table. "Well, if we're finished here, I got to get back uptown."

"You goin' to the club?" Black asked.

"Not right away, but I'll be there sometime tonight."

"I'll see you up there later. I wanna run something past you."

"Cool," Bobby said and left the restaurant.

After Bobby left, Black, Nick, and Wanda talked and had drinks. When Wanda excused herself to the ladies room, Black turned to Nick.

"There's somethin' I want you to do for me."

"What's that?"

"There was a robbery at Paradise Fish and Chicken. Two people were killed."

"Employees?"

"No, customers. They were standing in line when the bandits hit. Shot them for no reason."

"What do you want me to do?"

Black reached in his pocket and pulled out a fat envelope. "Take this to the family. The address is in the envelope. Her name was Zakiya Phillips; the money is for her grandmother. To help out with expenses."

Nick took the envelope from Black. "It'll give me a reason to get out of the house."

"With Wanda pushin' me to get involved in the legit side, I'll be busy most of the day," Black said and shook his head.

"You? Busy during the day?" They both laughed because Black was truly a night person.

"Picture that. But if that's where we're headed, she's right. I need to be on top of it; especially since that's where the most money is being made. So tomorrow, you call Kevon after you get done with Mrs. Phillips. I want to talk to you about some other things." Black told Nick as Wanda returned to the table. "About time. I was about to send a waitress in to check on you."

"I didn't think I had been gone that long. You must be ready to go?"

"Exactly," Black said and called for the check.

Nick didn't feel like driving back uptown, him and Wanda got a room at the Westin on 43rd Street. Once they had checked into the room and had gotten comfortable, Wanda had questions. "Did Mike ask you what you wanted to do?"

"I didn't tell him that I was thinkin' about runnin' the game if that's what you wanna know. But there is something he does want me to do."

"What?"

"Did you know that there was a robbery at Paradise Fish and Chicken?" Nick asked, knowing that she did. Wanda stayed on top of everything. There were times when he wondered who her sources were. He would make it his business to find out.

"Yes. I heard that a couple of people were killed. What does he want you to do?"

"Take some money to one of the victim's grandmother," Nick replied and waited for her to say something, but she didn't. Wanda just moved closer to him in bed and put her head on his chest. *Maybe I don't know her as well as I thought I did,* Nick thought. When she began gliding her hand over his chest, Nick knew then that Wanda wasn't interested in talking.

Chapter 6

Nick

The next morning Wanda left to go to her office, and I went back uptown and got ready to take the envelope to the victim's family. I understood from my army days what was in front of me. Having to tell parents that their child was dead wasn't an easy thing. This wasn't the same thing, since she already knew that her granddaughter was dead, but I still wasn't in the mood to deal with her grief. I had enough of my own.

When I got to Mrs. Phillips's apartment, I knocked on the door and waited for her to answer. It took a while, but finally the door opened. "Mrs. Phillips?"

"Yes." she smiled. "How can I help you, young man?"

"My name is Nick Simmons. Mike Black asked me to stop by and give this to you." I tried to hand her the envelope and get away from there.

"Mr. Black said to expect you. Come in," Mrs. Phillips said and stepped aside to allow me to enter the apartment.

Not wanting to be rude, not to mention having respect for my elders, I went inside. "Thank you."

Mrs. Phillips was slow getting around, but she led me into the living room and offered me a seat. "Can I get you something to drink?"

"No, thank you. I wouldn't want you go to any trouble," I said and tried to hand her the envelope again, but she wouldn't take it.

"Nonsense. It's no trouble at all. What would you like?"

"Whatever you have is fine."

"I just made a pitcher of iced tea, or would you like something a little stronger?"

"It's a little early in the day for me," I lied. Lately, I've been waking up to Johnnie Black.

"I usually have a glass of brandy around this time of day. One drink in the morning and one before bed, it's the secret to living a long life."

Since I wasn't about to argue with her wisdom, I accepted. "That'll be fine. Can I help you?"

"No. You relax and be comfortable," she said and disappeared into the kitchen.

When Mrs. Phillips returned with our drinks, she sat down in a chair by the window. "Come sit by me," she said and pointed to the chair closer to her.

"I want you to know how sorry I am about your granddaughter," I said as I came toward her.

"That's her in that picture," Mrs. Phillips said and pointed to a picture frame.

I picked up the frame. "She was very pretty."

"And smart too. Wasn't like so many of these young girls her age. Out there runnin' these streets, doing God only knows what. She was a good girl. Going somewhere, had a future ahead of her."

I saw a tear run down Mrs. Phillips face and I felt her pain.

"Do the police have any idea who shot her?"

Mrs. Phillips laughed. "Do they ever?"

"Not in this neighborhood," I laughed too.

"Zakiya called me that morning, like she always did. I mentioned that she didn't sound like herself. Zakiya was one of those bubbly kinds of people. Always smiling, always had something nice to say, but that day she just didn't sound right. Didn't sound like herself. She said that she was meeting somebody at that place and that she was a little nervous about it."

"Did she say what she was nervous about?"

"No, and when I asked her about it she just said it was nothing and changed the subject."

"What else did the police tell you?"

"They said it was drug related, but that's a lie. They said that the boy she was with was a drug dealer. They said those kind of people don't need a reason to kill; probably killed my baby for kicks or for some type of initiation."

"But you don't believe that, do you?"

"No. Zakiya would never be involved with drugs or drug dealers. I told you, she had her life planned out. Knew where she was going and was on the road to getting there."

For the next hour, Mrs. Phillips and I sipped brandy and talked about Zakiya. Naturally, she mostly talked and I mostly listened. Mrs. Phillips raised her after shooting heroin consumed her mother's life. Zakiya never knew her father.

Mrs. Phillips told me how Zakiya went out of her way to avoid drugs and not get in with *the wrong crowd,* so she could get an education. She was determined to be somebody, because she refused to turn out like her mother, a teenaged mother strung-out on drugs. Zakiya had a bachelor's in sociology with a minor in psychology. She was about to attend law school in the fall. "Does that sound like the type of woman who was involved in drugs?"

"No, it doesn't."

"You damned right it doesn't."

The longer I sat there, the more Mrs. Phillips reminded me of my grandmother. She raised me after my parents disappeared. One day when I was eleven they just didn't come home. No one really knew what happened to them. My younger brother and sister went to live with my aunt and uncle in Mississippi.

They didn't want me.

My uncle said they were just babies and they would raise them in the church. He said that I was into too much trouble and he was right. Those days I was into everything. After that, it was decided that I would go live with my grandmother, and I didn't see my brother and sister again. After awhile, it didn't matter as much. My grandmother was good to me. She showed me much love. She died five years later. But I had a new family by then.

About a year ago I went to Mississippi and tracked them down. My brother is a deacon in the church and my sister is married to the minister. I saw them, talked to them, but I didn't tell them who I was. They had no idea that they even had an older brother. They were two- and three- years old when I last saw them. I guess my uncle never even told them about me. Look how I turned out as opposed to them. Their brother: the gangster, the killer.

"You tell Mr. Black that I appreciate him sending you over to give me that money. I can't remember the last time I entertained a handsome young gentleman."

"I'll take that as a compliment."

"It was meant to be one." Mrs. Phillips smiled. "I'm not accustomed to taking money from people."

I stood up and put the envelope down next to Zakiya's picture. "I understand that, but please take it to cover funeral expenses and that type of thing."

"You tell Mr. Black if he really wants to do something for me, he will catch the people who took my baby from me. You promise me that, Mr. Simmons."

"Please, call me Nick."

"Promise me that you will find out who did this and see that they get what's coming to them."

"I can't promise you that, but I promise to do what I can."

"That's all I can ask for, Nick." Mrs. Phillips laughed. "It's more than the police offered me. To them it was case closed."

"Do you have a picture of Zakiya that I could borrow?"

She gave me a picture and told me where Zakiya lived. I left that apartment thinking that I probably wouldn't be able to find the bandits, but I would do what I could. One more thing to get me out of the house, and my mind off Freeze.

Chapter 7

Iwas up five o'clock that next morning, ready to go and out the house before Wanda opened her eyes. I wanted to be at the police station before the first shift came in. I needed to talk to Tamia Adams. She's a New York City police sergeant who used to provide information for Freeze. I wanted to see if she had heard anything about the robbery. I had to catch her there because she'd moved and I had no other way to contact her.

Tamia took Freeze's death very badly, much worse than his so-called woman, Tanya. So bad, that she cried through the whole funeral. After that, Tamia had to take some time off from work 'cause she was cryin' all the time. That's why she moved out of her apartment; said there were too many memories of Freeze there. Since then, any time she has something for us she's been talkin' to Black directly.

"Sergeant Adams," I said when I saw her walking toward the building. I guess I startled her 'cause her head snapped around. She relaxed a little when she saw it was me. Tamia gave me a hug and a kiss on the cheek.

"How you doin', Nick?"

"I'm good. The question is: how are you?"

"It gets a little better everyday."

"Is there someplace we can talk?"

"Not around here."

"I understand," I said and we went back to my car to talk.

"What's up?"

"There was a robbery at one of the businesses we own."

"Which one?" Tamia asked.

"Paradise Fish and Chicken."

"I know the place. Good take-out."

"Two people were killed."

"Your employees?"

"No, they were customers. They were standing in line. Apparently the robbers shot them for no reason."

"I haven't heard anything about that, but I'll ask some questions and get back to you." Tamia took out a business card and wrote her new address and phone number on the back of it. "Memorize that and get rid of it, please."

I started to go home and get back in the bed. Wanda and I had been up late and I was tired. I started driving in that direction, but somewhere along the way I decided to ride by Zakiya Phillips's apartment and have a look around. I didn't know what I was looking for, but I went anyway.

Mrs. Phillips didn't have a key to her granddaughter's apartment, so I let myself in. It was a small apartment, but it was very well-furnished. Zakiya seemed to have good taste; a taste for very expensive stuff. Mrs. Phillips didn't say anything about Zakiya having a job, just that she was a good girl, who had a bachelor's degree in sociology and a minor in psychology and was about to attend law school. I looked around the apartment and wondered what type of work-study program she was on that would allow her to afford the kind of stuff she had.

I could think of one.

Drugs.

Maybe Mrs. Phillips didn't know Zakiya like she thought she did. Wouldn't be the first time the parents were surprised by what their child was really into. I continued to look around for anything that would support my conclusion. If she really was involved with somebody who was involved in the game, maybe there were some clues here that would lead me in the right direction. The only thing I found was a picture that she took at some club, and a business card for a beauty shop.

I took both and left her apartment, and once again decided against goin' home and gettin' in the bed. The beauty shop was to be my next stop. I went in the beauty shop to ask if anyone knew Zakiya and could tell me anything about her. While the beauticians told me their stories about what a nice girl Zakiya was, and how they couldn't imagine why anybody would want to kill her, one of the customers, who was looking at me but not offering any comment, got up and left. "Where you goin', Dee? You're next," one of the beauticians said as she headed for the door.

"I just got to get something from my car. I'll be right back," she replied and left the shop.

I asked a few more questions and listened to a few more glowing endorsements about how wonderful Zakiya was, and then I left the shop. Before I made it to my car the woman stopped me.

"Hey mister."

"Yes," I said and walked toward her.

"You want to know about Zakiya?"

"I do. Were you and her friends?"

"Yeah, we were friends. We weren't real tight or anything like that, but I knew her. We used to hangout, you know, hit the clubs or whatever. I know her better than any of those bitches in there."

"Why didn't you say anything before?"

"I don't want any of them gossipy bitches up in my business. Other than them being here when Zakiya got her hair done, ain't none of them know anything about her."

"What can you tell me about her?"

"Not much. Like I said, we wasn't real tight. I'll tell you what I do know if it will help you find out who killed her. Just not right now. I gotta get back in there before I lose my place. I don't want to be here all day. Can I meet you sometime later?"

"When they're finished with your hair, I'll be right here in that car waiting for you," I said and pointed at the Caddy.

"You don't mind waiting?"

"Not if you got something to tell me, I don't," I told Dee and got in the car.

I don't know how long I had been waiting when Dee tapped on the window; probably 'cause I fell asleep as soon as I got comfortable in the car.

I motioned for her to come around to the passenger side and she got in. "So what can you tell me about Zakiya?"

"What you want to know?"

"Did she have a job?" was my first question. I really only had two.

"Yeah, she had a part-time job at Cross County Mall."

"Do you know where?"

"No. Just that she worked out there."

"Do you know if she was involved with drugs or anybody that sells drugs?"

"If she did, she never said anything about it. And I can

tell you for sure, when you got a baller on the hook, you tell everybody."

"Even if it ruined her good-girl image?"

Dee laughed when I said good girl. "Zakiya was cool, and I don't think she was rollin' with no ballers, but good girl—I don't think so."

"What makes you say that?"

"Good girls don't fuck married men."

"Do you know who this married man was?"

"No, she never would tell us what his name was or what he did. Just that he was married and had enough paper to take good care of her."

"But you're sure it wasn't a baller?"

"Sure? No. But Zakiya didn't have no heart for drugs. She never said why she was so against it, but she was. Her feeling that way, I seriously doubt that she would get involved with somebody like that."

"Thanks for your help."

"Can I ask you something?"

"Go ahead."

"Why you keep asking me about this drug thing?"

"Cops say her murder was drug related. Her grandmother doesn't believe it."

"Neither do I," Dee said and started to get out of the car.

"Where can I find you if I have anymore questions?"

Dee dug around in her purse for some paper and something to write with. She wrote down her number and handed it to me. "You can call me anytime; whether you got questions or not."

Chapter 8

Idecided to go by Paradise Fish and Chicken. On the way there I called Wanda's personal assistant to find out who the manager of Paradise was. She told me that his name was Al Harris, and she offered to call ahead so he would be expecting me.

The place was crowded when I got there, so I took a seat and waited for them to clear the line before I approached the two ladies behind the counter. While I waited I noticed the security cameras behind the counter and another one in the dining area. I wondered if they had a recording.

Once the line was gone, I stepped to the counter. "Hello, ladies. Is Al Harris here?"

"You must be Nick Simmons," one of the ladies said. She had light, almost blonde braided hair and light eyes, neither of which appeared to be her own.

"That's right."

"Al said we should be nice to you," light eyes said.

"Said we should treat you like we treated Freeze," the other said.

"How did you treat Freeze?"

"I was scared of him, but Shameka liked him. She thought he was cute," light eyes said, and Shameka took a playful swing at her.

"Tasheka?"

"What? You *was* always talkin' 'bout what a cutie he was."

"Yeah, but he don't need to know all that," Shameka said. "I'll go get Al for you."

"So you want somethin' to eat, somethin' to drink?" Tasheka asked. "I guess since we supposed to treat you like Freeze, everything is free. You can have anything you want," she said with her arms open as Al Harris came rushing out of the back. "Chicken is fresh out the fryer and I just made the lemonade."

"Lemonade sounds good, but don't put a lot of ice in it."

Tasheka smiled at me and went to get the lemonade.

"Mr. Simmons. I'm Al Harris, I'm the manager here," he said nervously. He was an older gentleman, in his late fifties maybe.

"Call me Nick," I said and shook his hand.

"What can I do to help you?"

"I wanted to talk you about the robbery and the people that got shot here."

"I was in the back, so I didn't see what happened. I told the police that. Tasheka and Shameka were both working; they can tell you what happened."

"I notice that you have cameras, do you have a recording of it?"

"Yes, sir. You could look at it in the back or I could make you a copy."

"Why don't you go ahead and make me a copy while I talk to the ladies. I'll look at the video after that," I told Al and he rushed off.

"So tell me what happened."

"Well, I was workin' the register and Tasheka was get-tin' the food when they came in."

"Where were the two people that got killed?" I asked.

"Right where you're standing," Tasheka said.

"Go on."

"They walked straight up here, pulled their guns, and one said 'give me all the money,'" Shameka said.

"The other one stepped up and shot them," Tasheka added.

"What did they look like?"

"They were both dark-skinned. They both had on base-ball hats, dark glasses and black scarves, so I couldn't see their faces," Tasheka told me.

"But one of them, the one that shot those people, had dreads," Shameka said.

"What happened then?"

"I gave them what was in the drawer, which was noth-ing but a hundred and fifty dollars."

"Good thing they didn't go in the back 'cause Al had just came and got the money out the register. They prob-ably woulda killed him too."

"Did either of the people say or do anything before they shot them?" I asked.

"Nope," Shameka said. "They was just standin' there waitin' to make an order. I was gettin' the money; they didn't have to kill those people."

"Could you tell if the two of them were together?"

"No. He came in first. She was in line behind him," Tasheka advised.

"You sure?"

"She be in here all the time. I never saw him before." Tasheka looked at Shameka. "You seen him before?"

"Not that I remember."

I showed them the picture that Mrs. Phillips gave me. "That her?"

Both ladies looked at the picture. "That's her," they both said almost at the same time.

"You ever seen her with anybody?"

"She meets some guy here, but it wasn't the guy who got killed," Tasheka said.

"If she was here he was coming. She always orders the food and be waitin' for him at a table," Shameka told me.

"Did you see him that day?"

The ladies looked at each other. "Nope," Tasheka said.

"I didn't see him," Shameka agreed. "Dag, you ask more questions than cops, don't he, Tasheka?"

"He sure does."

"Maybe I'm more interested than the cops."

After I thanked the ladies for their help, I went in the back to see what Al had for me. He handed me a disk and had the video cued up to the point where the bandits came in the place, then he left me alone in his office. I watched as it happened just like the ladies said it did. Watching made me wonder about something. I rewound the video and watched it again.

If neither Zakiya, or the other guy did or said anything to provoke them, why did they shot them?

The bandits were smart enough not to look directly into either camera. Then why risk a murder charge, over a hundred and fifty dollars?

It didn't make sense.

Not to me anyway.

Could the cops be right and Mrs. Phillips be wrong about Zakiya? The shooter stepped right up to her and put one in her chest. Then he shot the guy.

After I thanked everybody for their help, I assured them that I was going to get security up in there soon.

I left the restaurant and drove back to Zakiya's apartment. On the way there I called and left a message for Tamia Adams to call me. I wanted to know everything they had on the guy Zakiya was killed with. My thinking was that even though they didn't come in together, that this whole thing might be about him. But if that was the case, why did he shoot Zakiya first?

I had a lot of questions and hoped I could find answers in her apartment. There was one other thing I had to know about. Who was the man she usually met at Paradise? It was probably the married man that Dee told me she was seeing.

Once I let myself in, I went straight for her computer and went on-line. I searched her Internet history to find her e-mail provider. I hacked the password to her account; a trick my old partner Jett Bronson showed me. I began reading her e-mails and it wasn't long before I found an e-mail for somebody with the e-mail address nice_n_slow@msn.com.

In that e-mail Zakiya and whoever it was made plans to meet at Paradise. I sorted the e-mails by sender and read the next few. It was obvious from reading them that this was definitely the married man she was seeing. I printed the e-mail with the details and turned off the computer. I would take it to Monika to see if maybe she could find out the real name of the user or from where it was sent.

Chapter 9

On the way to Monika's house I thought about Jett. We'd all been a part of a special operations unit in South America killing drug dealers, blowing up drug plants and seizing their financial records. My specialty was weapons, commando tactics. Jett's specialty was electronic surveillance, computers; if it was high tech, Jett was on it. Monika's specialty was munitions. We were small teams, each working independently. But all of a sudden, the entire unit is needed to take out one plant. Then boom, everybody dies—except us.

The only reason we didn't die, too, was Monika fell on approach to the objective. Her ankle was broken and she couldn't continue. She wanted us to leave her, but Jett refused. "You can go if you want to, Nick, but I'm not leavin' her," Jett told me that day.

While Monika and I tried to lecture Jett on the need to follow orders and proceed to the objective, the objective blew up. I remember the three of us with our mouths wide open, watching it burn to the ground.

When I got to Monika's apartment, she looked surprised to see me. "I was just thinkin' about you," Monika said and shook her head. "Thinking about Jett really."

"That's funny. I was just thinkin' about him on the way over here."

"You know it's 'cause of him that I read the paper now." Monika pointed to the pile of newspapers in the corner. It didn't matter what country we were in, Jett always read the paper every day. "You never know what's goin' on unless you read the paper," Monika quoted Jett.

They were already the best of friends when I met them, although Jett thought Monika was mean, overbearing at times, and has a tendency to be a pain in the ass. And she held Jett personally responsible for the sins of the white man; they would do anything for each other. He's the reason why Monika is alive wearin' that patch and not dead. She had been shot five times.

The night that Monika got shot, I was at the hospital standing by the window watching the sunrise. When I turned around Jett was sitting there. He just sat there staring at Monika, he didn't even blink. I was worried because I'd never seen Jett like that before that night. Jett was always live. Finally, after about an hour, Jett said something. "I was there, Nick. I was right fuckin' there, Nick—Right there. She called me, Nick. She said things didn't go well with Chilly. She said to meet her at her house. When I got there I heard the shots. I ran to the door, yellin' for Monika. I went inside and saw her . . . lying there. I picked up the phone and called the cops. She tried to talk, but I couldn't hear what she was sayin'. I did what I could to stop the bleeding and make her comfortable. I heard a noise in the back. I got to the back door in time to see someone drive away. I got to my heap and I followed him. He didn't pick me up. He stopped at a house on 229th Street. I put on my gloves and went in after him. He didn't hear me come in; caught him in the bathroom pissin'.

"I popped him in the back of the neck and dragged him into the living room. I put him in a chair and tied him up. I slapped him around until he came out of it. I took out my knife. He tried to get free." Jett shook his head. "That wasn't happening. The more he moved the tighter the rope got. I asked him who he was and why he shot Monika, but he didn't answer, so I cut him. Just a little cut on the arm to get him bleedin'. But he didn't say shit. Didn't even flinch. I told him I would cut him every time he didn't answer me. He just looked at me. So I cut him again, but he wasn't talkin'. I worked him over pretty good, but the bastard wasn't sayin' shit. So I went back to cuttin' him. We had been there for hours, Nick. Blood was all over the floor. He was shakin' and shit. I was really fuckin' pissed when I saw the sun coming up. I walked up to him and cut his throat."

"You killed him?"

"That's what I just fuckin' said. I cut his fuckin' throat."

I remember sitting down in that hard-ass chair and burying my head in my hands. "Jett, you killed the only person who could tell us who tried to kill her and why."

"He wasn't gonna talk, Nick, so he had to fuckin' die. We don't need him to tell us shit, Nick. That fuckin' Chilly knows why."

And it didn't take Jett long to find out. He called me later that night. "I know who did it."

"Who?"

"I can't talk now. Meet me here."

"Jett, wait!" I yelled, but he was gone. I drove as fast as I could, but when I got to the house, Jett was gone. I drove down the street slowly. I saw Jett's car parked on my right. I parked up ahead of him and walked back to his car. I came around to the driver's side. "What's goin' on, Jett?"

"Jett!"

I looked in the car. His eyes were wide open. "Jett!" I shook him. That's when I saw the trail of blood coming from his ear. I opened the car door and Jett fell into my arms. He was dead.

He had been there for Monika. She called Jett, and his being there to stop the bleeding saved her life. He called me and I didn't get there in time. I thought about Freeze; another good friend that died in my arms because I wasn't there for him.

"Nick? You all right?"

"Just thinkin' 'bout Jett and Freeze. And don't tell me I need to let that go."

"I wasn't gonna. Hold on to that pain; embrace it. We need our pain. I think it makes us stronger."

"I think so too." I just hoped we were both right and the pain I felt from their deaths would make me stronger in some way.

"Now, what you need from me?"

"I really need Jett on this," I said and told Monika what I was into, what I found out, and what I needed her to do. When I told her, she laughed.

"You don't need Jett for that. You could have used any number of IP-address locators that are available on-line to find out where those e-mails were sent from," Monika said and opened her laptop.

"I didn't know that."

"Pay attention and learn something," she said and Googled IP-address locator and chose the first one it listed. "This is quick and dirty, but it will get you the information you want."

"Suppose I wanted to know where it was sent from and who the account belongs to?"

Monika closed her laptop. "That requires a little more work. This is only gonna tell me where the server is and who it belongs to. To get what you want, I'll have to hack into their system. This is where you need Jett."

"That's why I came to you. Can you do it?"

"Of course I can. I may not be as good as Jett, but I have skills too. Give me some time. I'll call you when I have something."

Chapter 10

I went back to my apartment and called Kevon. He said that they would pick me up in an hour. While I waited, I had a drink and thought about Freeze. I thought about how I was allowing my rage and guilt to consume me, and the effect it was having on every part of my life. I was drinking a lot more than I should and I knew that it was affecting my relationship with Wanda, if not our sex life.

I've been staying in my own apartment more than at the house with her. I was angry and irritable and though I try not to take that anger out on her, there are times when I know I do.

When Black got there, I jumped in the back seat of his Cadillac CTS. Black got in the back with me and we were on our way. "Did you take care of Mrs. Phillips?" Black wanted to know.

"I gave her the money and she said to thank you, but if you really wanted to do something for her, you'll find the guys who did it."

"Revenge."

"Yeah."

"How'd you leave it?"

"I told her that I couldn't promise her anything, but I'd see what I could do."

"What do you think?"

"Wouldn't hurt to ask around; see if anybody knows anything about it."

"I agree. How much did they hit us for?"

"Couple of hundred."

"Oh," he said. I thought Black was going to say that it wasn't gonna be enough money for him to want to invest any time in. "But I don't need people thinkin' that since Freeze is dead that it's cool to hit our spots, and we don't do anything."

"I'll take care of it."

Black nodded. "Good."

I guess "I'll take care of it" was the right answer.

"While we're on the subject, do you actually have a license for being a private investigator?"

"Yeah, why?"

"I was thinking about revivin' our old security company."

"Invulnerable. I haven't thought about that in a long time." When Black and Bobby went freelance and started doing jobs on their own, Wanda insisted that the first thing they should do was to start a business to run their money through. The name of their company was Invulnerable Security. Black chose a security company because it would give them a license to carry guns.

"Yeah, neither have I," Black said. "But Wanda got me thinking about legitimate business opportunities."

I laughed.

"What's so funny?"

"Nothing. Just trippin' on how she got us all."

"Yeah, well, when she's right she's right." Black looked out the window for awhile, and I wondered if he was trippin' on being legit. I knew I was. I was about to ask him when he turned to me. "Anyway—I was thinking about revivin' Invulnerable and hirin' some people and puttin' them to work in our cash businesses. You know, make our people feel more secure workin' there, maybe even provide a deterrent to little bullshit robberies like this. Get somebody to go around and get other businesses to take a guard at their spot. You know how we do it. If that works out, I was thinkin' that we could expand into private investigations too."

I laughed a little. "That's a damn good idea." Even though Black was thinkin' legit he was still gangster. *You know how we do it.* That meant you send a guy in and tell him they need a security guard and here's what it's gonna cost you.

"You get with Wanda and tell her to find out what it's gonna take and make that happen."

"I'll talk to her about it."

"I know Wanda has her own ideas about this. She wants you to take over the finance company. I know that ain't you. So have you thought about what you might want to do?"

"I was thinkin' about the game."

Black laughed. "Don't think Jackie can handle it, do you? I know Bobby and Wanda don't."

"How do you think she's doin'?"

"She got her boy Travis up there with her now."

"Which means?"

"Which means I'm not sayin' no to you. Not yet anyway. Give her a chance. Which means you check on the game every night."

"Just the game or do you want me to check on everything?"

Black looked out the window and didn't say anything

at first. Then he looked at me. "Freeze checked on everything."

"He definitely stayed on top of shit."

"Somebody needs to step up and do it. Everybody knows you. Everybody respects you. It should be you."

"Whatever you need, Black. You know that."

"Me and Bobby been talkin' about this and I was gonna talk to you 'bout it."

"About what?"

"I need you to run things."

I looked at Black and didn't say anything. I was only talking about running the game. I didn't know if I was ready or if I even wanted to run the whole show. But how could I say no to him. "Like I said, Black, whatever you need."

"We can start makin' this happen tonight. You ride with me tonight. We'll roll by our key people, the earners; you know what I mean. Let everybody know you run the house now."

Just like that.

The first person we saw was Howard Owens. He was a bookie who did a little loan sharking. Howard had been with Black from the days when Black first separated from André. He was a good earner.

"What's up, Black?" he said and turned to me. "What's up, Nick?" He looked in Kevon's direction and nodded. "How you gentlemen doin' on this beautiful New York day?"

"I'm good, Howard. What's up with you?" Black asked.

"Let me holla at you for a minute, Black," Howard said and started to walk away. Black motioned for me to follow them.

When Howard noticed that I was walking with them, he stopped. "It's okay. Say what you gotta say."

He went on to explain that he had loaned a guy named Charles Watson fifty thousand dollars to expand his construction business and now the guy was ducking him for the last two months. After he gave us all the information he knew, Black turned to me.

"What you think, Nick?"

"I'll put a couple people on it," I said and looked Howard in the eye.

"From now on, if you have any problems you see Nick. Understand?"

Howard nodded his head and we walked away. And that was that until we got back in the car.

"Here's what's gonna happen with Mr. Watson. We're gonna checkout his business and see if it's something we're interested in. If it is, you're gonna tell him to forget about the money and then make him see how it's to his advantage to give us—" Black thought for a second. "I'm not gonna be greedy, say ten percent of his company."

That's how the entire day went. Everywhere we went, everybody we saw, all of them had an issue that they wanted Black to handle. I imagined that it had been awhile since some of these people had seen Black, 'cause some of them had a list.

Black would sit and listen and then he'd turn to me and ask the same question. "What you think, Nick?" And every conversation would end the same way. "From now on, if you have any problems you see Nick. Understand?"

Once we were back in the car, Black would tell me if he agreed or disagreed with the solution that I proposed. If he didn't, he would tell me what I should do. "Use your best judgment for the little shit," Black said. "If it's something major, play them off and we'll talk about it."

Between stops, we spent most of the time talking. Black talked a little about the future according to Wanda, but then he turned to the other side of the house. How he saw things now that Freeze was gone, and how he wanted things to go; ideas he had and ways to accomplish it.

When Kevon parked in front of Clay's garage, a chop shop run by a guy named Bo Freeman, we went inside. "Wait here," Black said and walked up to Bo.

He and Bo walked off together and then Bo stopped. "What?" he said loud enough that everybody in the place looked at them. Bo looked back at me; tried to stare me down. I looked him in the eye. I knew if anybody blamed me for Freeze's death, it was Bo. Freeze brought Bo in, taught him the game. It was Freeze who put Bo in this spot. I knew I would have to watch him.

Black put his arm around Bo. Whatever he said, Bo shook his head and Black walked away. "Let's go," Black said to me and Kevon and headed for the car.

As the night rolled on we had seen just about everybody who could be found. Kevon rolled up at the game I thought I'd be takin' over.

It had been awhile since I'd been there, so there were a few faces that I didn't recognize. I looked around for Jackie and Travis, while Black made his way around the room.

I was about to knock on the door to the office when Jackie opened the door. "Hello, Jackie." I must have caught her off guard, 'cause she was about to reach for her gun. I put up my hands.

"What's up, Nick?" Jackie asked and relaxed.

"I'm good. How's it goin' tonight?"

"For the most part—" That's when she saw Black on the other side of the room. She smiled and started walkin' toward him. "It's been a good night. Lost a little early, but its breakin' back our way. Other than that, I'm good."

"Where's Travis?"

Jackie looked at her watch. "He'll be here in a little

while," she said, when she got to the spot where Black was talkin' to Sonny Edwards, one of the regulars at the house. "Good evening, Mr. Black."

Black looked up at her, nodded his head, and went back to his conversation. Jackie folded her arms and stood there. Since she seemed content to stand there and wait for him to get through talkin' to Sonny, I went and joined Kevon at the bar.

I had been at the bar talkin' to Kevon, who is a pretty funny guy when he does talk, which isn't very much, when I looked around for Black and didn't see him. Since I didn't see Jackie, either, I figured they were in the office, and I should be in there. "I'll be right back," I said to Kevon.

"No need. Jackie *'dem* know you boss now," Kevon said and raised his glass to me.

At first it felt funny hearing him say it; *you boss now*. I was having a hard time accepting it, but as the day went on, it became more and more apparent to me.

Somebody needs to step up and do it—it should be you.

Suddenly I felt powerful, and for the first time I really thought about what that meant and whether I wanted to carry that type of power and responsibility. It really didn't matter at that point. It wasn't like I was about to tell him no. If that's what Black needed, then that's just the way it was.

The last place we went to was Cynt's. She ran a strip club that had gambling in the basement, and has for years. Historically, Cynt's had always been one of my favorite spots. Naked women have always had a haunting pull on me.

Cynt, who had an ass that just wouldn't quit, started out dancin', doin' a little trickin' as most of the dancers did, and had developed a reputation for the things she could do with her mouth. It was a skill that attracted Bobby's attention back in the day. That all ended when a customer roughed her up pretty bad, and she quit and swore that she would never do that again.

After she recovered from her injuries, Black, being loyal to his people, put her to work behind the bar. As time went on Black noticed that she had other skills that proved to be more useful to him and when the opportunity presented itself, he put her in charge of the spot.

Unlike everybody else we saw that day, Cynt had no issues. She had been around long enough to handle her own issues, and Black felt comfortable enough with her to let her handle them anyway she saw fit.

"From now on, if you have any problems that you can't handle," Black told Cynt, "which I know you won't, talk to Nick."

"You know I can handle mine," Cynt said and then she turned to me. "Congratulations, Nick. I'm happy for you. If you ever need anything, you let me know."

"I will."

"See that you do," Black recommended to me. "Cynt can be a big help to you."

The three of us had been talking for awhile when I noticed one of the dancers who called herself Mercedes talking to Kevon. Trying to get past him really. She had been staring at Black the whole time we were talking to Cynt.

Once we were done with Cynt, Black signaled to Kevon that he was ready to go. I followed Black to the door, but when I turned back, Kevon seemed to be having problems separating himself from Mercedes. When we got in the car and were on our way, Black tapped Kevon on the shoulder as he drove.

Chapter 11

Mike Black

"What she say?"

"Her say she can't understand why I am trying to keep her from you. That I know you want to see her," Kevon said. "Her think I must be working for Miss Maria and not you."

I laughed. "She'll be all right."

Then I turned my attention back to Nick. "It's all you now. I know I can count on you. From here on out, you and I need to talk at least once a day. And if you don't mind, for the time being, unless it's a legal matter, I want to keep Wanda out of the loop. I don't need her thinking that you have to report what's goin' on to her. If she has a problem with it you tell her that's the way I want it and she can talk to me. I know she ain't gonna wanna hear that shit."

Nick laughed. "She'll be all right."

Nick didn't say anything else on the way to his apartment. Probably thinkin' 'bout what he had in front of him. I knew I put him in a tough spot, but I also knew he could handle it.

Once we dropped Nick off at his apartment, I told Kevon to call Maria. We were going dancin' at Impressions, and I wanted her to be ready when we got there for a change. But I knew when I got there she still wouldn't be ready. She never was.

Maria used to dance at Cynt's, where she went by the name Mystique. She'd been dancing at Cynt's for years and I always marveled at how much she looked like Cassandra. I ran into her about a month after Cassandra died. At first, I thought my mind was playing tricks on me. Maria was bigger than Cassandra: five-eleven and heavier, but there's not an ounce of fat on her. Her complexion, lips, facial structure, and her eyes; she had the same beautiful eyes. There are still times when I wondered if Maria and Cassandra could be sisters. Could she be one of Chicago's many children? Maria never met her father and her mother was dead, so there was no way I would ever know for sure.

"Nick say anything about Jackie?" After Freeze was killed, it was a couple of days before I got around to checkin' things out. When I got to the game, there was Jackie holdin' it down. Since she'd been watching Mylo for me, Jackie knew how things worked. Everything was goin' fine. I owed Jackie for puttin' me on to Mylo. And besides, I respected the way she stepped up and ran the game when I needed her, so I left her there.

"He start to come in the office, but I tell him, Jackie 'dem know you boss now."

"What he say then?"

"Nothing. Him lost in thought after that. We drink and wait until you come out."

"Lost in thought, huh?" Yeah, I know, I shouldn'ta just dropped it on him like that. I shoulda talked to him about it, made sure he understood what I wanted him to do. You know, made sure he wanted to do it. But you know what? Either he'll step up to the job or he won't. If things had happened the way they were supposed to, it would have been Nick runnin' the day-to-day operations when me and Bobby made the decision to take a less active role.

If Bobby hadn't threatened to kill him over Camille, he would have never joined the army. I would have chosen Nick over Freeze. Not that I had a problem with Freeze or the way he ran things; it woulda just been Nick's time.

When we got to Impressions, I found Bobby at the bar surrounded by women, as usual. "What's up, Bobby?"

"Chillin'," Bobby said and dismissed the women he was talkin' to. "How you doin' tonight, Mystique?"

"I'm fine, Bobby."

"Yes, you are," Bobby said to her and then turned to me. "You and Nick do y'all's thing today?"

"Just dropped him off."

"And?"

"He'll be all right."

"Come on, there's somethin' I need to talk to you about."

"I'll be right back, Maria," I said and kissed her on the cheek. "You want me to leave somebody with you?"

"No, Kevon is around here somewhere."

I followed Bobby to his office. As we made our way through the crowd, it seemed like he knew every woman we passed—Waving to him, blowin' kisses and shit. "I thought you were gonna call me today," one woman said.

"I thought so too," Bobby said and kept walkin'.

"What happened to you last night?" another asked.

"That was so long ago that I don't remember," was his answer.

"Am I gonna see you later?" asked a woman in a red dress.

"I never make plans that far in advance," Bobby told her and dismissed her.

Lately, Bobby's head hasn't been on business. He's been in some kind of early mid-life crisis, or some shit like that. He brought a new CLK350 Cabriolet convertible Benz and went back to runnin' the club, which he didn't really have to do since Tara has been runnin' the joint for years. I mean he's still with Pam and he's a good father to his children, but he's on a mission to fuck as many women as he can. I can't say shit about that 'cause I've been on a tear my damn self.

In addition to Maria, and the occasional stray, I fucked Mercedes. The day after I'd made Maria stop dancin' at Cynt's, she set the pussy out for me. To be honest with you, I really don't even like her. Probably 'cause she got 'bout as much sense as a box of rocks, but she is so fuckin' fine that I had to have her. The last time we were together she told me that she was gonna change her name to Diamond, 'cause when I call her box of rocks she thinks I'm talkin' 'bout diamonds.

Then there's Jackie's fine ass. Jackie is bi-sexual and likes to invite her girlfriends along to play with us, which always makes for an interesting night. And Jacara; she's a nightclub singer that I met in the Bahamas. I only see her when I'm down there visiting Michelle.

Maybe it's both of us in mid-life crisis.

I know Bobby loves Pam and would like for things to be different between them, but it is what it is. I know what my problem is. I love Cassandra and I miss her. Miss everything about her. The hole she left in my life has grown, and no matter how I try to fill it with these women, I know I never will.

When we got to the office, Bobby made us some drinks while I went and stood by the two-way mirror that overlooks the club. I looked out on the floor for Maria and spotted her on the dance floor. I looked around for Kevon, he was on the dance floor too, but his eyes were on Maria.

"What you wanna talk about?" I asked when Bobby handed me my drink.

"I want to know what direction you goin' in."

"What you mean?"

"I mean you got Wanda wide-open; making plans for us to get out of the game and at the same time you got Nick steppin' up to run things."

"What's wrong with that?"

"Other than it makin' for some long nights in that house, you mean?"

"Yeah, other than that."

"Nothing, I guess. I just wanna know where your head is."

"One is the future, one is the past."

"I know that shit. Wanda's in my ear with that shit all the time."

"Right now, as long as we're makin' money and no-body's fuckin' with us for a change, I don't see any reason why we can't do both. But us goin' legit is where we're goin'."

"Fair enough. So what y'all got planned for me in this bold new world?"

"I don't know. What you wanna do?"

"What Wanda got you doin'?" Bobby asked.

"Goin' to borin'-ass meetings with borin'-ass people talkin' a bunch of borin'-ass shit that I only half understand. But the numbers look good, so I ain't sayin' nothin'. Wanda is makin' us a chunk of money that way."

"Any women at these borin'-ass meetings?"

"Some."

"Probably a bunch of stuck-up hoes who think they're better than everybody."

"Some are, some aren't," I said and thought about Meka Brazil. She's a very smart and very interesting investment banker who Wanda and I met with about a week ago. Sometimes I wonder why I'm attracted to powerful, professional women like her, but gravitate to woman like Maria and Mercedes.

"Well, next time you have one of these borin'-ass meetings, I want to be there. If that's where we're goin' in the future, I need to be a part of it."

"I got no problem with that. Tomorrow afternoon we got a meeting with some real estate agent. Wanda wants to buy some warehouse and office complex in Long Island. It's your money too; you should be involved. I really didn't think you were interested in shit like that."

"I'm not, but if times are changin', I need to change with them."

"I'll give Kevon the day off. Come get me around noon."

"Cool." Bobby laughed. "And you can tell Wanda that I'll behave."

"Whatever, Bob," I said and got up.

Chapter 12

When we got back to the club the first person I ran into was CeCe. She used to be with a baller who called himself Cash Money. He was murdered by Mylo's hit team. Since then, she has been tryin' to get with me by making herself useful, which she was, very useful at times. I tell her to do something and it's done. But I still avoid her 'cause CeCe is a statuesque beauty, who has the type of raw sexuality that makes men fall at her feet, which makes her a very dangerous a woman. "Hey, Bobby."

"How you doin', CeCe?"

"I'm good, Bobby," CeCe said to Bobby but her eyes were on me.

"Oh, yeah, I forgot to tell you . . ." Bobby said. "CeCe been lookin' for you, Mike."

"Thanks."

"No problem," Bobby said and walked away.

"Hello, Mr. Black," CeCe said with that sugary voice that always makes me want to rip the clothes off her body.

"What's up, CeCe? You look nice tonight."

"It's a Diane Von Furstenberg lipari dress. You like?" CeCe asked and stepped closer to me.

"Yes, I do. But you look good every time I see you."

"Which isn't often enough, but I love it when you like what I wear. You know I pick my outfits with you in mind. You liking what I wear makes it worth the money I paid for them."

CeCe was in the apartment when Cash and his crew got popped. Before the police got there, CeCe took all the money and dope out of the place and left it with one of her neighbors. She sold the dope and kept the money.

Smart girl.

"How'd you know I'd be here?" I asked.

"I've been looking for you, but I know you know that. I know you always show up here sooner or later. But I see you got your woman with you tonight, so I won't disrespect her and take up a lot of your time, but I do need to talk to you about some business."

I looked at CeCe for a second and then I turned and unlocked the door that led to the office. I stepped aside to let her pass and locked the door behind me.

"So this is what's behind the black door. You know everybody wants to know." CeCe went up the stairs that led to the office and I gladly followed behind her. When we got to the office, CeCe walked to the window and looked out at the club. "I always thought that this was a two-way mirror."

"See how smart you are."

"I'm glad you noticed."

"Can I get you a drink?"

"I'm fine."

"You don't mind if I do?"

"Of course not," CeCe said and sat down on the couch.

I fixed my drink and sat behind Bobby's desk. "What business you need to talk to me about?"

"You still looking for that guy Mylo?"

"What about him?"

"I saw him on the news a couple of weeks ago. His name was really Clint Harris and they said that he was a DEA agent, but it was the same guy. They found him dead in Philly."

"I heard that too. What about him?"

"Well, you remember when you said you were looking for Mylo and I said I didn't know who that was?"

"I remember."

"Well after I saw him on the news, I remembered that he used to come by the apartment to see Cash."

"But you knew him as Clint Harris and not Mylo?"

"That's what I've been tryin' to tell you."

I sat there for a second or two thinking before CeCe said something. "What?"

"If Cash knew his real name, did he know that he was DEA?"

"How could he not know? I mean, it could happen, but I doubt it."

"How well did you know Mylo or Clint or whatever his name was?"

"Not well at all. I told you I hadn't been with Cash that long. Clint used to come by the apartment sometimes and they'd talk."

"What they talk about?"

"They would always ask me to leave, so I never did know or really care what they were talkin' about, but what I could hear was Clint tellin' Cash how he could handle things."

"Why you care now?"

CeCe looked at me like she couldn't believe I actually had to ask her that question. "Why you think?"

"Enlighten me. This way we'll both know."

"You. I'm diggin' you, Mike Black. I think I've made that plain. I know you here with your woman. She's a very pretty woman and I hear she's good people, and y'all got your thing, whatever it is. And believe me, I do respect that, but the fact of the matter is I want you. And you know what's funny?"

"What's that?"

"I know you want me."

"What's funny about that?"

"What's funny is I can't figure it out. I know you want me. I can see it in your eyes when you look at me. I can hear it in your voice when you talk to me. I can tell it by the way you avoid me unless you need something from me. And don't try to say that you don't avoid me, 'cause we both know it's true. 'She'll be all right.' I believe that's *your* line."

She was right. That's exactly what I say anytime somebody tells me that CeCe was lookin' for me. When I didn't comment, CeCe continued.

"And you gotta admit, when you need me, I come through for you, don't I?"

"You do."

"Every time. And you're gonna need me again and I got you, baby. Anything I can ever do for you is done. But I need you to understand something."

"What's that?"

"I do what I do for you 'cause I want to. I want you to know the kind of woman I am. I understand that since I used to be with Cash that you didn't trust me, but I hope we've gotten past that. I want you to know that you can trust me, and you know that you can depend on me to handle mine and whatever you need me to do. I want you, Mike Black; want you bad and I want you to want me the same way. That's why I do the things that I do for

you. Not 'cause I know you'll break me off something. I don't need nothing from you, I got my own." CeCe took a breath. "Oh, I didn't tell you, I'm getting ready to open a high-end boutique in a couple of weeks. So bring your woman by and I'll hook her up."

I knew why she threw that in. By now CeCe must have heard that I bought a gym for Maria to run. Since she was a personal trainer, I thought it was a good match for her since I made her stop dancin' at Cynt's.

"Let me know when you open and I'll drop by." I thought about legitimate business opportunities for the future. "Depending on how you do in business, I may want to talk about investing in your expansion."

"Partners with Mike Black, I like the sound of that. It will make me work that much harder."

I bet it will. "My name ever come up in any of these discussions between Cash and Mylo?" I asked, switching the subject back to business before I said something that would take this conversation in a direction that I wasn't willing to take it. But CeCe was right about me. I do want her; wanted her bad. Every time I see her, she makes me want her even more. Then why do I avoid her? Maybe it's because I haven't wanted a woman like this since I met Cassandra, and I wasn't ready to feel like that.

Not now, maybe not ever.

"Nope, I would have told you by now if I had heard your name. Him and K Murder used to talk about you all the time. Talk about you like you was Darth Vader."

I laughed. "No one ever compared me to Darth Vader before."

"How you know?" CeCe said and stood up. "You don't know how these niggas in them streets are scared to death of you."

"I guess I don't."

"That's why you got me to let you know these things.

And you do got me, Mr. Black, all of me. I'm just waiting for you to take me." CeCe started walking toward the desk. "I know you got to get back to your woman. She's probably looking for you and giving Bobby a hard time about where you are."

I picked up the phone and called Kevon on his cell. "Yes, boss."

"Come to the office."

"On my way," Kevon said and hung up.

I got up and led CeCe to the door. "The least you can do is give me Kevon's number."

I went back to the desk and wrote it down. I handed the paper to her. "Thank you. I promise not to blow it up." CeCe looked at it then looked at me. I felt that urge to rip her clothes off as Kevon knocked on the door.

I opened the door for Kevon. "Escort the lady out and tell Bobby I need to talk to him."

"Well, I guess this is goodnight, Mr. Black."

"We'll talk again, soon."

"Is that a promise or a threat?" CeCe remarked as she closed the door behind her.

I walked over to the couch and sat down. I sat there thinking about what CeCe had just told me about Cash and Mylo. Did Cash know Mylo was DEA? If he did know, how did Vinnelli fit into this?

Chapter 13

Nick

Iwas tired when Black dropped me off. I had gotten up early that morning and it had been a long day. I decided not to fight it any longer and got in bed. I woke up to the sound of my cell phone ringing. "Hello," I said, but I was still half asleep.

"Nick, its Tamia. I got something for you."

"What you got?"

"The way I hear it, the murders were drug related and the robbery was just a cover."

"That the official line?"

"Pretty much, but I heard some talk that the robbers might be associated with a gambler named Jasper Robinson, calls himself J.R."

"Thanks, Tamia. If you hear anything else let me know."

"I will," Tamia promised and hung up the phone.

I rolled over and tried to go back to sleep when I heard somebody knocking on my door. I thought about ignoring it, but got up anyway. I got my gun and went to

the door. I was about to see who it was when I heard the
key hit the lock.

The door opened and Wanda stepped in.

"Hello."

Wanda jumped. "You scared me." Then she saw the
gun. "Were you gonna shoot me?"

"Yes," I said and turned around and headed back to
bed.

"You all right?"

"Just tired," I told her and got back under the covers.

"Too bad," Wanda said and began getting undressed.
"You been with Mike all day?"

"No. I took some money to Mrs. Phillips. I spent the
day lookin' into the murder at Paradise. I was with him
most of the night."

"Did Mike ask you what you wanted to do?"

"I told him that I was thinkin' about runnin' the
game."

Wanda frowned. "What did he say?"

"Black said to give Jackie a chance; said she got Travis
up there now."

"What good does he think Travis being there, knowing
less about the game than she does, is gonna accomplish?" Wanda asked, questioning Black's logic.

"Security. I didn't ask him. He wants me to check on
them every night."

"Just the game?"

"No, Black wants me to check on everything."

"Anything else he want you to do?" Wanda asked without commenting on what I had just told her—which surprised me. Maybe she didn't understand what everything
meant. But knowing Wanda, she just wanted to know
everything before she said anything about it.

"No, that's it."

"Okay," she said and headed for the shower.

Once she got out of the shower and dried off, she got in bed. When Wanda rolled close to me and kissed me, I thought we were getting ready to have sex, but Wanda had other ideas. "I have to be honest with you, I'm not sure I like the idea of you checking on everything."

Now it comes.

"I didn't think you would."

Wanda rolled her eyes at me. "I mean, I can see where this is goin'."

"Where do you see it goin'?"

"He's got you taking money to that family, something Freeze used to do. You're going to start making the rounds every night, something Freeze used to do. Black wants you to take over."

"That's exactly what he wants. But you have a problem with it?"

"Frankly: yes. Yes, I do. You know that I think that we need to be moving away from all that, not have you move into Freeze's spot. But I guess Black has other ideas about what we should be doing." She folded her arms across her chest.

Wanda is so fuckin' sexy when she pouts.

"Black understands that we need to be moving in that direction; and he said that he is taking more of an interest in our legit business."

"Did he say that, or are you just guessing?"

"That's what he said, especially since we're making more money on that side. But he understands that right now, we are still in the business and somebody needs to stay on top of that."

"I agree."

"I'm glad you do,"

"Why you? Why can't him or Bobby do it?"

"Because you got him busy gettin' up on the legitimate business, and Bobby, I guess you need to ask him about that."

"I will. But why you?"

"Why not me? Don't you think I can handle it?"

"That's not it and you know it."

"Then what?"

"I don't want to lose you, Nick. Don't you understand that?"

"Of course I understand that."

"But that is not gonna stop you from doing it, is it?"

"No, it's not. If that's what Black wants me to do, then that's what I'm gonna do."

"I knew he was just playing me off with all that shit about how we gonna get out and make up that income."

"I don't think so."

"What makes you say that?"

"Because I think he wants to get out. He's lost a wife; I know he doesn't want this to touch Michelle."

"I should have been prepared for him; anticipated him asking that. Next time I'll be ready."

"If you were paying attention, he gave you the answer to both questions."

"What do you mean?"

"You have everybody buy us out and then you take that money and flip it. Invest it in shit that will make up the income. But I guess you weren't paying attention."

"I guess I wasn't."

"Too busy pouting."

"You love these pouty lips," Wanda said and pushed them out.

"Yeah, I do, so I tell you what I'm gonna do."

"What's that?"

"While I'm making the rounds, I'll feel everyone out on it. When we think the time's right, I'll bring you around with me and you can run it by them, establish a price and then we'll go to Black together."

Chapter 14

Jasper Robinson.

I knew J.R. from the old days, but I hadn't seen him in years. Him and André were friends, used to run together. He owns a nightclub called J.R.'s and he ran a poker game, scraps, the usual stuff, in the basement at night. I would roll by there later tonight.

After I checked on a few of our stops, I stopped by J.R.'s. It was still early when I got there, a few people; probably regulars seated at the bar. I took a seat and signaled for the bartender.

"What can I get you?"

"Johnnie Black on the rocks."

When the bartender came back with my drink I hit him with my question. "Is J.R. here?"

"Who?"

"J.R., the guy who owns this place, is he here?"

"You a cop?"

"Nope. Old friend."

"Wait here," the bartender said and came out from behind the bar. He took another look at me before he went in the back. It wasn't too long after that when I was approached by two big muthafuckas.

One tapped me on the shoulder. "Who you here to see?"

I turned around on my barstool. "Jasper Robinson. Calls himself J.R., owns this place."

The other man looked at me. "I know you, don't I?"

"I don't know. Do you?"

"Yeah, you're Nick Simmons, you work for Mike Black."

"That's right."

"I'm Jeff Ritchie," he said like I should know the name. He looked disappointed when I said, "I don't know you, I just want to talk to J.R., is he here?"

"Yeah, he's here. Follow me."

Jeff Ritchie led me in the back to the office and he knocked on the door. When J.R. answered, Jeff Ritchie stuck his head in. "Somebody to see you, J.R."

"Who?" J.R. asked and I walked in. "Nick, Nick Simmons."

"What's up, J.R.? How's it goin'?"

"Not bad for an old man. What about you? I heard that you were back in town. I haven't seen you in what—fifteen years?"

" 'Bout that."

"Come on in, have a seat. Can I get you a drink?"

"Johnnie Black on the rocks."

For the next hour, J.R. and I sat in his office and talked about the good old days and I drank his liquor.

"Young bucks these days don't respect nothing. No respect for the game, no respect for each other," J.R. said.

"Tell me about it."

"You know what the problem is, Nick?"

"I know you're about to tell me."

"There was a time when you had to be brought into

the game. You know, the way André brought Black in, and then he reached out to you and brought you along. You learned the game that way; learned that there were things that you just didn't do. Men had respect for one another. Now, shit, any dumb nigga with a couple of dollars he can rub together can get him a package and bam, there he is. Dumber than a muthafucka; not knowing shit, but how to pull his gun and shoot over stupid shit."

"Times change, J.R. After awhile there won't be a place in the game for things like honor and respect," I said and thought that this would be a good time to talk about what I came here for. "While we're on the subject, J.R., there is something I need to talk to you 'bout."

"You know, Nick, I been in this game a long time, which means I know enough to know that you ain't come here just to drink my liquor and talk 'bout the old days."

"I meant no disrespect."

"What's on your mind, Nick?"

"Last week there was a robbery at one of Black's businesses. Place called Paradise Fish and Chicken. Two people were killed."

"I hadn't heard anything about that. Now I'm wondering *why* you wanna talk to *me* about this?"

"My sources tell me that the bandits were connected to you."

"I see. How much money was taken?"

"About two hundred dollars."

J.R. laughed. "Nick," he said and tried to stop himself from laughing. "You have to excuse me for laughin'. I didn't mean you any disrespect. I know this is a serious matter, or you wouldn't be sittin' here. But I can assure you that I had nothing to do with it. I ain't about to fuck with Black over chump change."

"And believe me; it's not about the money. Two people

were killed, civilians, just standing in line waiting for their food. That type of thing is bad for business."

"I understand."

"To be honest with you, J.R., I don't believe you knew anything about it, 'cause if you did, the people involved would be dead for bringing that kind of weight on you for that little bit of money. But the word is out there that it was your people. All I'm asking is that you ask some questions."

"You have my word on that, Nick. If I find that it's true, I'll call you before I put a bullet in the back of their heads," J.R. promised and I took him at his word.

Chapter 15

Just then, there was a light knock at the door, and it opened slowly. A young woman walked in. She was attractive, if not pretty, but she had a body that screamed LOOK AT ME!

J.R. sprung to his feet, so I stood up too. Besides, I had said what I came here to say and I was ready to go.

"Sorry, Daddy," the woman said. "I didn't know you were busy. I'll come back later."

"No, no. It's all right, Lorraine. Come in. I want you to meet somebody."

She went and stood next to her father and I could see the resemblance.

"Nick, this is my daughter Lorraine. Lorraine, this is Nick Simmons, he's an associate of Mike Black."

Lorraine smiled like somebody told her that she had just hit the number. "I've heard a lot about you, Mr. Simmons. It's an honor to meet you."

"It's Nick, and it's good to meet you too, Lorraine."

"Call me Rain," she said and went to the bar to fix herself a drink. "I'm just gonna get a drink and then I'll be out of your way. We can talk later, Daddy."

"It's good that you're here, Lorraine. Nick was just tellin' me that one of his places was robbed, and the word is that we had something to do with it. You hear anything about that?"

"Nope," Rain said quickly. "How much money we talkin' 'bout here?"

"About two hundred dollars."

Rain laughed just like her father did. "I can tell you right now that we wouldn't be involved in no small-change robbery like that."

"All the same, Lorraine, I want you to talk to Jeff Ritchie about it and ask around. Two people were killed: Innocent people, just waitin' to get their food." J.R. turned to me. "See Nick, this is exactly what we was just talkin' 'bout. There was a time when something like this would never happen. Killin' civilians over some chump change, shit, every player in town would be all over this, tryin' to make it right 'cause it makes all of us look bad," J.R. said angrily.

"I knew you would understand, J.R. I've taken up enough of your time. If you hear anything let me know," I said and started moving toward the door.

"I'll do that, Nick. You have my word on it." J.R. turned to Rain. "See Mr. Simmons out, would you, baby, and tell Jeff Ritchie that I need to see him."

Rain kissed her father on the cheek. "I'll see you later, Daddy."

Rain looped her arm in mine and walked with me out of her father's office. As we passed the bar Rain turned to me. "You in a hurry, Nick?"

"Not especially."

"Good. Then you have time to have a drink with me."

"Sure," I said and Rain led me to a table near the back of the club and signaled for a waitress.

I had Johnnie Black of course, she had straight tequila. After we ordered, Rain took a deep breath. "I wasn't exactly honest with you back there in the office."

"Honest about what?"

"The robbery."

"What about the robbery?"

"I heard the same thing. That it was some of our people that did it."

"Why didn't you say that then, and the better question is why are you tellin' me now?"

"You probably couldn't tell it to look at him, but my father ain't in the best of health. He's been sick a lot lately."

"I couldn't tell. What's wrong with him?"

"Doctors don't know. Bunch of fuckin' quacks. All that fuckin' money we give them and other than him havin' high-blood pressure, they can't tell us shit."

Rain stopped talkin' when the waitress returned with our drinks. Once the waitress left, Rain shot her tequila. Not wantin' to be punked by this young girl, I shot mine.

"I don't like to bother Pops with shit like that. I ain't tryin' to make his pressure go up. You see how upset he was gettin'."

"I can understand that. But my question is what you gonna do about it?"

"I can take you to the place where they hangout."

"I don't need you to take me anywhere. You just need to tell me who they are and where to find them."

"No deal."

No deal?

Has this little girl lost her fuckin' mind?

"What you mean no deal? This ain't no fuckin' negotiation. You're gonna tell me what I need to know and I'll take care of it."

"Good luck findin' them without me then."

I had to admit, the little girl had heart, I just wasn't gonna admit it to her.

"Look, Nick, if these are my people, I'm the one who needs to make this right. Not you, me. So here's how it's gonna go. Me and you gonna roll by they spot, and I'm gonna handle my family's business. And I'ma tell you why. See, I ain't no stranger to you and how you handle your business."

"Really?"

"Really. Niggas is still talkin' 'bout some of the shit you and that nigga Freeze used to do: Burnin' bitch-niggas with acid and shit; throwin' muthafuckas off rooftops and shit. Y'all was the type a niggas that would shoot first and never get to the ask questions part. See, if you do that, all it's gonna do is make muthafuckas wanna bust back for they homies. Then y'all gonna come at us and that ain't how this shit need to go. Am I right?"

I didn't answer her 'cause she was right. The way I was feelin', I wouldn't be askin' how and why. I might just walk up on whoever it was and put a bullet in their brain and we'd be at war over some bullshit when Black, not to mention Wanda, are making plans to move us away from all this.

"Okay." I stood up. "We'll do it your way."

"I knew you'd see the logic in my point," Rain said and started for the door.

We got in my car, she told me where to go and I headed in that direction. I started to call some people to handle this shit for me, you know, since I was boss now. But I wanted to do this myself. I needed to let out some of this rage I was feelin' over Freeze being dead and it being my fault. And besides, I was the one who promised Mrs. Phillips that I would see that whoever killed Zakiya would get what's coming to them.

On the way, Rain told me about the stories she had
heard about me and I told her which ones were true. "I
gotta admit that I always wanted to meet you. I met
Freeze a couple of times. That was one scary nigga, may
he rest in peace; and relentless. Once he was on to something, you might as well lay down 'cause you was good as
dead."

The more she talked about me and Freeze and the way
we used to roll, the madder I got. I tried to calm myself
down by changing the subject. "So with J.R. being sick,
and you keepin' shit from him, who runs things? Jeff
Ritchie?"

"No. Jeff Ritchie is a bullet. You load him in a gun and
pull the trigger. Jeff Ritchie ain't got the mind for shit like
that."

"The question still stands."

"I run shit."

"You?"

"Yeah, me. Somethin' wrong with that?"

"How old are you?"

"I'm twenty-two. And in case you didn't hear me the
first time, I'll ask you again, is somethin' wrong with
that?"

"No. Ain't nothing wrong with that, as long as you can
handle it."

"And you don't think I do?"

"I don't know you. And even if I did, I still wouldn't
give a fuck. How y'all run your business don't matter to
me."

"Okay, Nick. Chill out. I wasn't tryin' to make you mad
or nothing. I got mad respect for you. And if what I hear
in the wind is true—then you ain't the one to be fuckin'
wit'," Rain said.

I took a breath. "So, why don't you tell me how you
run your thing?"

"Well, Pops still pretty much runs the gambling and shit. And I run everything else."

"What is everything else?"

"Little of this, little of that. I usually got something goin'. Sell a little dope, you know."

"I thought J.R. wasn't involved in the dope game?"

"He ain't, and he don't know that I am. And I hope that you ain't plannin' on tellin' him. Like I said, shit like that will just send his blood pressure through the roof, and I ain't havin' that."

"You don't have worry about me bein' a snitch. But I seem to remember J.R. havin' a son. What's up with him?"

"My brother Miles. He's playin' the family-man role. You know, he's married, and got a couple of kids. He runs the club and keeps the books. He ain't got no heart for this other shit."

"Okay, Rain, why don't you tell me who we're goin' to see?"

"His name is Rodney Baker, but they call him Shake."

"You know why he robbed our joint or why he killed those people?"

"I ain't heard nothin' 'bout that. I just heard it was him and his crew. I was gonna see 'bout it, but me and Shake don't usually see eye-to-eye on shit. That's what I was gonna talk to Pops about. Get some advice on how to settle our beef."

"I thought you didn't wanna bother him with shit like that?"

"I don't. But that nigga is all out of control."

Chapter 16

We pulled up in front of the place and went inside. It was a neighborhood joint, long bar and a few tables. Loud rap music pumped from two huge speakers at the back of the room. "You see them?" I asked and Rain took a quick look around.

"No."

I looked the place over for other exits. Always a good idea to know how we were gonna get out in case shit gets wild. "You know if that door leads to the street?"

"I think it goes to the back door that leads to the alley. But I ain't sure."

"Why don't you get us a table by that door? I'm goin' to get us a drink."

I went to the bar and ordered while Rain went to find us a table. The bartender had just put our drinks on the bar when three men came through the front door. I looked over at Rain. She nodded her head and started moving through the crowd to get to them.

"That's fifteen," the bartender said.

I peeled off a twenty. "Keep the change." I shot my

drink and started for them. As I made my way, I saw Rain get up in the face of a big Jabba the Hut lookin' mutha-fucka. I assumed that he was Shake by the size of his belly. By the time I got to them I heard Shake say, "You beat me outta ten grand, bitch!"

"Who the fuck you callin' bitch, you fat muthafucka? I ain't beat you outta shit!" And with that, Rain reached back and slapped the shit outta him.

Jabba the Hut came out with his gun. I already had mine out. Rain was a little slow with hers, so were Jabba's crew. They were still trippin' off Rain bitch-slappin' Jabba.

Since I wasn't tryin' to kill him, I hit Jabba in the arm with my first shot, but that didn't stop him from shooting at Rain. The people in the place all scattered at the sound of the shots.

Rain turned over a table and took cover. Then she sprang up quickly and fired a few rounds at Jabba. He was a big muthafucka, so there was no way she could miss his big ass. She caught him with one to the gut and one to the head. Jabba went down hard.

While the crowd forced their way out the front door, I grabbed Rain by the hand and headed out the back. We made it back to my car in time to hear the police sirens in the distance.

Rain was hyped as we drove away from there. "That's what I'm talkin' 'bout! Did you see the way I slapped the fuck out that nigga, the way I put two in his bitch ass?"

"Yeah, Rain, I saw it." Maybe it was her first time, I don't know, but she definitely was more excited about it than I was.

"When we do catch up with the niggas that robbed you, I'ma do the same shit."

"What you mean? That wasn't them?"

"Nah. I asked him 'bout that before we got into it 'bout our shit."

I was mad as hell, but I tried not to show it. "You believe him?"

"No reason for him to lie 'bout it."

"I heard him say that you beat him outta ten grand."

"The muthafucka say the package I sold him had so much cut on it that he couldn't do nothing wit' it."

"Was it?"

"Why you wanna know all that?"

"Why you think?"

"Damn. Sorry I got you up in that shit." Rain laughed. "He was right, the shit was stepped on. But that's not how I usually roll. He just caught me at a bad time."

"So instead of making it right, you killed him for it." This was exactly the kind of shit her father was just complaining about. If J.R. knew his daughter was out here, not only dealin', which he is dead set against, but doing shit like this.

"Hey, I tried to make it right. When he came at me 'bout it I offered to make it right on the next package. But he said he wanted his ten Gs back. I said give me back the dope. Nigga says he cooked it up and sold it. Now what am I supposed to do?" Rain asked and I didn't bother answering her. She wouldn't have liked my answer anyway. There was silence until we pulled up in front of her father's spot. "What we doin' here?"

"What you think we doin' here? I'm droppin' you off."

"Why?"

"You got anymore ideas?"

Rain folded her arms across her chest and her lower lip eased out a little. She had just shot somebody and now she was pouting like a spoiled child.

"I didn't think so."

"Well, where you goin'?"

"I got shit to do."

"Let me ride wit' you?"

"For what?"

" 'Cause I may know somebody who might be able to put us on to them." Rain reached for the door handle and opened the door. "But if you're too busy to handle your business. I'm gone."

"Shut the door, Rain."

She closed the door and I drove off.

Chapter 17

Who the fuck does this little girl think she's tryin' to play? Since I was the only other person in the car, I guess she thought she was playin' me. Only question was, whether or not I was gonna let her think she was gettin' away wit' it. Truth was I needed her right now. I wanted to put this thing behind me and move on. "But this better turn out to be something."

"I can't promise shit at this point. I just dropped the muthafucka I thought it was. Only thing I can tell you is that this nigga Nacho, he be hearin' shit. Maybe he heard something 'bout your thing."

"Nacho Marquez?"

Rain's expression changed. "Yeah. You know him?"

"No, just the name." I'd heard Freeze mention him a few times. He told me that Nacho was a bookmaker and a gambler who made a reputation for himself for having information for sale. At least I knew that Rain hadn't beat him on weak product. But there was something about the way her expression changed when she thought I might know Nacho that bothered me.

For the time being, I put that aside, but at the same time I understood fully that Rain had her own agenda working here, and I was a part of it. That meant I should be ready for whatever. "Where we find him?"

"You in a hurry?"

"Yeah. I told you, I got shit to do. I don't have all night for this shit." I stuck my finger in her face to be sure she got the point. "So if your boy Nacho can't tell me shit, I'm done with you. If the muthafuckas that robbed my joint belong to you, and you wanna put your house in order, that's cool. You call me when you put a bullet in their brains."

"Look, nigga, I'ma say this one more time. Only muthafuckin' thing I can tell you is that this nigga Nacho be hearin' shit. Now if that ain't good enough for you then pull this bitch over and let me out. I'm tryin' to help your muthafuckin' ass and you givin' me shit 'bout it."

I stopped at the next red light. "You can get out now. I'll find Nacho without you," I told her calmly. Rain didn't reach for the handle this time.

When the light changed I drove on. "So where we goin'? And yes, I'm in a hurry."

"Co-op City. Section four."

"Anything I need to know about you and Nacho?"

Rain shook her head.

We drove to Co-op City, which is located in the Baychester section of the Bronx, close to I-95 and the Hutchinson River Parkway. It's the largest cooperative housing development in the world. If it were a municipality instead of part of Bronx, it would be the 10th largest city in New York State.

We got to Nacho's building and went in behind one of the residents. We took the steps to Nacho's floor and knocked on his door. It took awhile before a male voice came back from the other side of the door. "Who is it?"

"It's Rain. Open the door, nigga!"

"Go away!"

"Oh—so it's like that, huh?"

Rain started bangin' and kickin' the door until he opened it. When he did, Rain stuck her gun under his chin. "Go away, my fat ass," she said and took his gun from his waist. "Now, where's Nacho?"

The man pointed.

"Well move then."

He started walking backwards slowly, and Rain kept the gun pressed to his chin. I followed her in. For a young girl, Rain could definitely handle herself. As we got closer I could see that there were three men seated in the living room.

"Who's at the door?" one of them yelled.

Once we were in the room one of the men started to reach for his gun, but the other one stopped him. I assumed that he was Nacho. "What do you want, Rain?"

"What's up, Nacho?" Rain said and pushed the doorman to the floor. He looked at me and started to get up. I shook my head and showed him my gun. He decided to keep his spot.

"Get off the floor, you look ridiculous," Nacho said. He looked at me one more time to make sure it was all right before he got up. "Now, what do you want, Rain?"

Rain went and sat across from Nacho with her gun on her lap. "I don't want nothin'. Maybe I just came to holla at you, Nacho. You know, since we cool and shit."

"Yeah, Rain, we cooler than a fan. Now what the fuck do you want?"

"See how you treat a sistah? That shit ain't even necessary." She looked at me. "Why can't muthafuckas just get along?"

I don't know what she was lookin' at me for. I agreed with Nacho. I wanted her to get to the point too.

"Like I said, I don't want nothin', but this man here, he got a couple of questions he need to ask you."

Nacho looked at me. "Who are you?"

"That ain't important. Right now, all you need to know is that I'm the one askin' the questions." I said and slowly reached in my pocket. I pulled out a wad of bills and that got his attention.

"What you wanna know?"

"There was a robbery at Paradise Fish and Chicken a couple of days ago. You know anything about that?"

"I heard about that. Couple of people got shot." Nacho looked at my roll again. "But as much as I hate to say it, I can't say who did it."

I put my money back in my pocket. "If you hear anything, you tell Rain. It'll be worth your while."

"If I hear anything about it I'll let her know, for sure."

Chapter 18

When I turned to leave, Rain stood in front of Nacho. "Say goodnight, muthafucka." She pointed her gun and put two in Nacho's head. "Rude muthafucka."

Then she turned and shot at the one sitting on the couch near Nacho. But he moved a little too quickly for her. The other man in the room pulled his gun, hit the floor quickly, and fired at me. I hit the floor and returned fire, but he had clawed away. I looked for Rain; she was runnin' down the hall chasin' the doorman and the one she'd missed. "I got them," she yelled and ran down the hallway.

I stayed low and made my way into the kitchen. I stood up to get a shot off, but he shot at me, and I ducked back in the kitchen. I held up my weapon and shot back blindly.

I could hear shots bein' fired. I yelled for Rain, but she didn't answer. I peeked around the corner and saw one running for the door. I hit him in back before he got out. I stood over him and put two shots in his chest.

There was still shooting going on in the back. I kicked

his gun away and started moving toward the hallway. I heard footsteps coming at me. It was the doorman, only now he had a gun. Rain came out of one of the rooms behind him. I aimed and fired at him, and he went down from one to the head. I kicked his gun out of the way as Rain walked slowly toward me.

"You all right?" I asked and Rain stopped right in front of me.

She was breathing hard.

So was I.

I could feel my heart pumping blood through my body and for the first time since Freeze died, I felt good. Felt alive.

"Yeah." I could tell that Rain felt it too. I should see it, it was written all over her. She was practically glowing.

"Any more back there?"

"No. I got his ass."

"We should go. Come on."

Rain and I left the building the same way we came in, down the stairs and out the front door with a group of residents. We took our time walking to my car; neither of us said a word until we were out of Co-op and on I-95.

Rain let out a deep breath; it was more like a moan. "Hmmm." Like the experience was almost sexual to her. It wasn't that good for me, but I did need to get some of the rage that I was feeling off of me.

I was starting to like Rain.

I didn't trust her, but I was definitely starting to like her. But I wasn't about to tell her that.

I was more interested in finding out why we just wiped out Nacho and his crew. "You wanna tell me what just happened?"

"Family business, Nick. Nacho was a snitch and had to be dealt with."

"You need to come a little better than that, Rain."

"You mind if I smoke?"

"Go ahead. Just tell me why we—and I do mean we—why we just killed Nacho."

Rain lit a cigarette and rolled down the window. "I had to take care of him for my father."

"What does J.R. have to do with this?"

"A couple of days ago, my father told me that he was worried about Nacho."

"Why?"

"He said that Nacho called and wanted to come by to talk 'bout the money he owed him. Only Nacho don't owe Pops no dough."

"What did J.R. think he really wanted?"

"He thought Nacho was tryin' to set him up." Rain took a deep drag from her cigarette. "You see, my father is a silent partner in a porno flick company with a guy named Paul Gaggiano. Well, a couple of weeks ago, Nacho was there to see one of the chicks in the movie. The cops raided the set and Nacho gets arrested along with everybody else."

"Was your father there?"

"No. But Jeff Ritchie was. Jeff Ritchie is a freaky fuck. He goes there all the time to watch. He was arrested too. But Nacho was back on the street before Jeff Ritchie even got his one fuckin' call. You know what I'm sayin'?"

"Nacho gave the cops something."

"What he gave up was my father. That's why I had to do this and not him. Jeff Ritchie is hot now."

"Go on."

"Pops began to suspect that Nacho had folded under pressure. Nacho's a weak-ass bitch, you know the type, can't do the time. So he told the cops that both my father and Jeff Ritchie were involved in gambling and were extorting money from him."

"How do you know this?"

"Pops may be a step or two slower, but he still got his sources. They was tellin' Pops that Nacho hadn't signed anything official, but he had more than one meeting with the cops. Bottom line, the bitch needed to be dealt with."

I didn't know if I believed her or not, and I wasn't sure if I really cared. If I really needed to know if she was lyin' or not, I could check her story with Tamia Adams or even her father. "I'm sure that J.R. will be relieved that you took care of that for him."

"He would, but he don't know and I got no plans of tellin' him. Both him and Jeff Ritchie are at the club with plenty of witnesses. They don't need to know nothin' 'bout this. All they need to know is that the bitch nigga is dead and he ain't no threat no more. End of story."

"That the way you want it?"

"That's the way it's gonna be. 'Cause I hope you ain't plannin' on tellin' him nothin' 'bout what happened in these streets tonight. This between you and me. Cool?"

"You askin' me or tellin' me?"

"Honestly, Nick, it's both."

"Don't worry, Rain. Your secret is safe with me. You don't need to tell anybody, and I mean anybody, that I was involved in any of this in any way. This between you and me. Cool?"

"Cool."

"I don't need any of this coming back on me and it lookin' like Black had anything to do with this."

We drove for awhile in silence. I needed Rain to think about how me backin' her up on settlin' her business, could drag Black and our whole organization into a place where none of us needed to be. We were supposedly moving toward getting out, not backin' Rain in whatever plan she had to consolidate her position. Me ridin' with her and backin' her play makes it look like that was exactly what we were doin'.

I looked over at Rain; the way the street lights hit her face. I really hadn't paid much attention to the fact that Rain was kinda cute. The fact that she was all gangsta wit' it made her sexy.

"Look, Rain, I understand that you had to handle your business, but why involve me?"

"My dog got cracked a couple of days ago, and the way it's lookin', he's goin' down for a long time. I knew I couldn't do this alone, so I needed a road dog to ride with me. Then you walked into my life and I knew that there wasn't nobody better at this shit than you."

"You coulda asked me."

"Nigga, please. You woulda asked me if I had lost my mind and told me to go away little girl."

"You're right, little girl, I would have."

"See."

"You lied to me."

"That's not *exactly* true. I didn't lie to you. I'm for real 'bout that. Yeah, I used you to get my shit done, but I did hear that Shake was in on the robbery, and Nacho. Since Shake say he didn't have nothin' to do wit' it I thought he could really put you on to the right people; for a price of course."

"Of course."

"So we good?"

"Don't ever lie to me again."

"I don't like the fact that you keep callin' me a liar, but under the circumstances, I'll let it pass for now. Let's get a drink and talk about it."

"I told you, I got shit to do."

"That's cool, but you still need to know who hit your spot, right?"

"Right."

"So let me help you."

"Why, you got somebody else you need to kill?"

"Fair question. But no. I handled all the family business tonight."

I pulled up in front of her father's spot and put the car in park. I took out a pen and wrote down my cell number. "If you hear anything that I can use, call me."

"I will, you can count on that." Rain got out of the car and leaned in the window. "I might call you; even if I don't have nothin' but some sweet talk for you."

Rain walked away from the car and I watched her swing that big ass until she went in the club. I thought for a second about having more than a drink with her. Then I put the car in drive and drove away.

I might have told her no, but part of me wanted to. Like I said, I was startin' to like Rain. I respected the way she saw what needed to be done and took care of it. There was a time when I might have done the same thing and worried about the truth later.

Chapter 19

Mike Black

I looked at Maria as she slept. She seemed to have a smile on her face and I wondered if she was dreaming, and if she was, was she dreaming about me.

When I do dream it's always about Cassandra. Truth is I think about her all the time. It doesn't matter where I am, who I'm with, or what I'm doin', I can't get her off my mind. I think about what my life would be like if she were still apart of it. I think about the sound of that sexy voice of hers dancing in my ear. I think about how her eyes seemed to come alive when she saw me. I think about how at every step I made decisions that led to her death.

I thought about my own nightmares. I don't have them as much as I used to, but every once and awhile I do. It always begins different, but it always ends the same way. I'll be dreaming about being with Cassandra, and we'll end up back at our house. No matter what I do to try and stop him, Kip Bartowski, the man who beat and murdered Cassandra, kills her again. Then I wake up in a cold sweat. It reminds me that everybody who was involved in her murder isn't dead.

But not tonight.

Tonight my mind wasn't on Cassandra. Tonight my mind was on CeCe.

I got out of bed and walked toward the window. I thought about our last conversation. She said Cash knew Mylo by his real name. Cassandra had a friend named Juanita that worked for the DEA in Washington.

I had her do a little digging and she found out that Clint Harris was a DEA agent and Kenneth DeFrancisco was his last supervisor. The way she got it was that after DeFrancisco went to jail, the agency lost track of Agent Harris, until they found him dead at his house in Philly. Fortunately for me, they had no idea what he was working on, or I would probably be in jail for his murder.

But that started me thinking about how long these bastards been on me, how deep they had infiltrated my house. It made me realize there was more to this than just DeFrancisco ordering Cassandra's murder and me being framed for it; that's just how it ended up. This was all part of Diego Estaban's plan for me.

Now maybe I'm paranoid, but I wondered just how deep this plan was? Killing Diego didn't stop it. DeFrancisco going to jail didn't stop it. He still had Cassandra killed. I thought killing DeFrancisco would put an end to it, but suppose it doesn't? Pete Vinnelli was still alive and pulling the strings.

The more I thought about it, the more the pieces fell into place. Mylo or Harris worked for DeFrancisco. DEA Agent Masters worked for Vinnelli. Logically, he had to know about their plan to kill me and for Mylo to takeover the Commissions drug markets. That meant that Vinnelli had his hand in it.

I had to know.

In spite of my promise to Angelo that I would let it go, I had to know. I had to know what their plans were, and try to get a feel for what else they may have in store for me. This was a crucial time for us, making the move to go legit. I didn't need this shit coming from nowhere to bite us in the ass. I had to be ready. I had to be a step ahead of them. I had to kill Vinnelli.

It was and still is the only way for Cassandra to rest in peace.

The next afternoon me, Bobby, and Wanda met with the real estate broker, and then she had a meeting scheduled at her office with Meka Brazil, the investment banker that we've been dealing with. The meeting was to discuss with us the financing ideas, equity, and bond issues.

At the meeting Meka recommended a very aggressive strategy for taking over some smaller companies, merging with others to form a larger company, and selling the company's stock to the public. At this point, we had no plans to tell her how we made our money, but she's smart, so if she hadn't figured it out for herself, at some point she will.

Then Meka started talking about us buying or investing in an insurance company that was looking to use derivatives to reduce risk in its investment portfolio. "I don't mean to sound stupid, but what are derivatives?" I asked Meka. I could tell that both Wanda and Bobby were glad that I asked 'cause neither of them had a clue what she was talking about.

"Derivatives are financial instruments whose value changes in response to the changes in underlying variables," Meka answered without appearing to be annoyed by my question. "The main types of derivatives are futures, forwards, options, and swaps."

"In English, please."

"Derivatives can be based on different types of assets

such as commodities, stocks, bonds, interest rates, exchange rates, or indexes. The main use of derivatives is to reduce risk for one party. The diverse range of potential underlying assets and pay-off alternatives leads to a huge range of derivative contracts available to be traded in the market. Their performance can determine both the amount and the timing of the pay-off."

"Thank you, for clearing that up for me," I said even though I still had no clue what she was talking about.

After the meeting was over, instead of rushing off to her next appointment, Meka came and sat down next to me.

"Mind if I ask you a question?" Meka asked.

"Not at all." I thought she was about to ask where the money came from, but I was wrong.

"Did you really understand my explanation of derivatives?"

"To be honest with you, no, I didn't. You might as well be speaking Latin."

"I didn't think so. But if I'm going to continue working for you, I think it's important that you understand what I'm doing on your behalf."

"I agree."

"That means that you have to understand what I'm talking about so you can make informed decisions about your company's future. Not just going along with what Meka says because she sounds good saying it."

"I couldn't agree with you more. The question is what are we going to do about that, Meka?"

"If you like, and your schedule permits, we could spend some time together and I could explain some of the basics of business investing."

"That sounds like an excellent idea. Naturally, you can present a bill for your time," I said, wanting to, as Wanda would say, at least give the appearance of professionalism.

Meka looked at her watch. "Look at the time. I have less than an hour to make it to a lunch meeting." Meka got up and gathered her papers. "But any time you want to get together and talk finance, just give me a call," she said and handed me another one of her cards.

"I'll do that."

Chapter 20

After Meka left, Wanda said she had a client coming and needed to prepare for it. Bobby, who had been talking to Wanda while I was talking to Meka, stood up to leave. "What you gonna do now, Mike?"

"Why; what you got up?"

"I was thinking about rollin' by Cuisine for lunch and then going by Cynt's."

"You go ahead, Bob. I got something I need to do."

"Does that something have anything to do with Meka Brazil?"

"No. Just some loose ends I need to tie up."

I didn't like keeping things from Bobby, but like Angelo, he thought leaving Vinnelli alone was the best thing for all of us. I didn't need him knowing that killing Vinnelli was back on top of my list of things to do. So him ridin' with me where I was going wasn't about to happen.

My next stop was the apartment of Monika Wynn. She used to work with Nick while they were in the army and for awhile after they got out and were playing private detective. She helped Jackie uncover what Mylo and Masters were up to.

"You want me to go in with you, boss?" Kevon asked me when we arrived at her apartment.

"You relax, Kevon. I got this one."

Kevon got out of the car and stood by the door while I went inside and rang the bell. It didn't take Monika long to answer. "Well hello, Mr. Black. This really is a surprise."

"Hello Monika. I need to talk to you about something," I said and wondered if I was interrupting her or if maybe she was expecting somebody else. She was wearing a Knicks throwback jersey, and as far as I could tell nothing else. Nick said his old partner Jett Bronson used to call her lips, tits, and hips.

She was definitely all those things.

Monika had a patch over her right eye. While they were investigating Chilly and that whole synthetic crack nonsense, she got shot five times; two shots in the chest, and two to the head. One hit her above the left ear. She caught the other one in her eye. They weren't able to save her eye. The other one was in her hand.

"Mind if I come in?"

"Sure." Monika stepped aside and let me in. "This must be important if you're here yourself."

"It is. I want you to do something for me."

"What you need, Black?"

"Information and discretion."

"Two things I'm good at." Monika came and sat down across from me. It gave me a chance to admire the way her nipples pressed against her throwback. "What's up?"

"Pete Vinnelli. I need to know everything there is to know about him. Everything. I wanna know where he lives, who his friends are, where they live and what they do. Who and where he hangs out."

"You still thinking about killing him?"

"That's where that word discretion comes in."

"I understand. But I'm way ahead of you," Monika said and got up. I watched her walk.

"You are?"

When she sat back down she had her laptop and a disk with her. "When all this came down, Nick asked me to start diggin' into Vinnelli. You know, looking for the best way to take him out."

"Really." I had to remember to thank Nick. It confirmed for me that I had made the right choice in putting him in charge of the house.

"I haven't had much luck following the money. After DeFrancisco went to jail, he got careful and tried to clean up his shit. He left enough of a trail for me to follow, but so far, every time I think I'm on to something, it hasn't led anywhere."

"Stay on that for me. I need to know where the money is and how much there is."

"I put my observation about his patterns, both business and personal, in this file. There're pictures and a little bit of detail on his two girlfriends." Monika handed me the pictures she had. "An Amanda White, divorced, mother of two, age: thirty-nine. And that one is Pamela Connote, she's twenty-seven."

"They kinda look alike."

"To me, Pamela is just a younger version of Amanda. Both got blonde hair, blue eyes, big tits."

"Man knows what he likes." I couldn't say shit since I was with Maria because she looked like Cassandra.

"Anyway, my report includes what I thought was the best way to kill him." I looked on as Monika copied the file to a disk and handed it to me. "You look that over and let me know what else you need from me."

"I need you to stay on finding that money," I said and

got up thinking about what I could do with a woman like her. She was a munitions expert, trained in weapons and commando tactics.

The perfect assassin.

"Drop by Cuisine later tonight and I'll have something for you." I started to leave but then I stopped. "By the way, Nick doesn't need to know anything about you giving me this."

"That's where that word discretion comes in."

"I knew I could count on you."

"I'll see you tonight," Monika said and walked me to the door.

"Thanks again for this," I said and held up the disk she had given me.

"Not a problem," Monika said as I walked toward the door. "Drop by anytime," she added in a voice that made me a little curious.

"Is that an invitation?"

"Yes. You can come by and see me anytime."

"What 'bout you and Nick?"

"There is no me and Nick, Mr. Black. Me and Nick served together in the army. We were partners. Nick is like a brother to me."

"He's like a brother to me too. I guess that makes us *like* brother and sister?"

"No, I don't think so," Monika shook her head and said.

"Why is that?"

"I tell you what, Mr. Black. If you really wanna know, you'll come back when you got some time and I'll explain to you exactly why you and I can't be *like* brother and sister." Monika opened the door and kissed me on the cheek.

"I just might have to hear that."

"See that you do."

Chapter 21

My next stop was to see Bruce Stark, who was once the head of a group of drug dealers that called themselves The Commission. It was formed as a buying co-op. When Detective Kirkland first told me about them I thought it was funny. "What are they; a rap group or something?"

He had confirmed from his sources that Cash Money Blake, K Murder Murdock, Billy BB Banner and Bruce Stark, were all lieutenants of a player named Birdie. Thinking that Birdie and his partner Albert Web were involved in Cassandra's murder, Nick and Freeze eliminated them while I was in jail. But Kirk told me that the sole purpose of the group was formed to protect themselves against me. The ability to buy at a cheaper price was nothing more than a byproduct.

After I found out the truth about Mylo, me and Stark made peace, and he was the one who told me where I could find Mylo after he shot Freeze. Since then, Stark and I have developed a kind of respect for one another.

Kevon drove me to Stark's apartment, which always

amused him. You see, Stark was a very security-conscious man ever since two members of his Commission, Cash Money and K Murder, had been murdered by Mylo and Masters' hit team. Maybe he thinks they're still out there, I don't know.

"Here we go, boss," Kevon said as we turned down Stark's block. First, there's a girl taking pictures of every car that comes down the street. When we parked the car and got out, four guys approached me.

"Here comes the welcoming committee," Kevon said. "All of them are pussies, yah know."

I laughed. "Be nice. They're just doin' their job."

"I know that, boss. But it take four of them?"

"Strength in numbers, maybe."

"Pussies," Kevon repeated and spit at the feet of the first one that got to us. "Mr. Black is here to see Mr. Stark."

They stopped askin' us to give up our guns since it wasn't gonna happen and they escorted us inside the building. There are two men in the lobby and another four in the hallway; two more at the elevator and one at each of the stairwells. The man takes his security seriously.

"What's up, Black?" Stark asked and shook my hand. He led me in the back so we could talk privately.

"There's something I need your help with."

"Me?" he actually seemed excited about the fact that I was coming to him for help. "What can I do to help you? Fuck that, as much shit as I come to you with, whatever it is, you just say it and it's done."

"Nothin' for you to do. I just need some information about Cash Money and Mylo."

"What about them?"

"You know Mylo's real name was Clint Harris and he was DEA?"

"Yeah, it was on the news when they found his body."

"Did you know that Cash knew him by his real name?"

Stark sat up straight. "No, I didn't know that." It took a second or two before the implications of that revelation hit him. "That means that Cash knew he was DEA."

"That's what I wanted to ask you about. First off, did you know?"

"No," Stark said quickly and looked around the room. "I swear 'fore God, I didn't know nothin' 'bout that."

"I didn't think you did, but I had to ask and see your face when you answered."

"Where did you hear that Cash knew who Mylo really was?"

"I have my sources."

"Can't be nobody but CeCe." Stark looked at me for a second. "Mind if I ask you a personal question?"

"You want to know if I trust her."

"Do you?"

"I haven't decided yet. Any reason you know of that I shouldn't?"

"No. Not really. I guess I'm just not a trustin' mutha-fucka, that's all. I'll say one thing for her, when Cash got smoked she was smart enough to get Cash's stash out of that apartment before the cops got there."

"I heard that too. You know who she sold it to?"

"Me."

I already knew that, I just wanted to see if he would tell me. "That's what I thought." I stood up and walked to the window and looked out. "No, I haven't decided whether I trust CeCe or not, but whether I do or not, I still need to know what the deal was with that and how it ties into some other shit I got goin'."

"What's that?"

I didn't answer him 'cause my business with Vinnelli was none of his fuckin' business.

"You know, now that I'm thinkin' 'bout it, the first time

Birdie introduced us to Mylo, Cash did say that he thought he knew him from somewhere."

"Yeah, Cash knew he was DEA."

"What you gonna do now?"

"I don't know," I said 'cause I didn't. "But if I need you to do something for me, I need to know if I can count on you."

"Whatever you need, Black."

I shook Stark's hand and left the building with Kevon. Cash definitely knew who Mylo really was. That's why Mylo hit Cash first. The logical thing would have been to take out Stark first. That would have sent The Commission in disarray. As we drove away from there I thought about what I was gonna do next. I needed to talk to somebody who could tell me more about Vinnelli, and I knew exactly who that was.

Chapter 22

Nick

I woke up the next morning to the sound of my cell phone ringing. I didn't know what time it was, but whatever it was, it was too damn early. When the phone stopped, the doorbell started, and then my cell started ringing again. "Okay, I get it; you're at the door," I said a loud and to nobody. I rolled out of bed and grabbed the phone. "What?"

"Come open the door."

It was Black. I looked at the clock. It was ten 'til ten. What the fuck was he doin' up, first of all; and why was he here so early? I opened the door for Black and Kevon.

Black came inside wearing a suit and a tie. He hates ties. Kevon nodded his head, turned around, and folded his arms. I closed the door.

When I got in the living room, Black was at the bar making a drink. Kind of early—but what the fuck.

"Pour me one too."

I sat down and Black brought me my drink. He sat down and smiled. "Did I wake you up?"

"Yeah, yeah you did," I said and laughed a little.

"I know it's early, but shit, I'm up. You might as well be up too."

"Thanks." I raised my glass and drained it.

"I'm gonna be busy the rest of the day and I wanted to talk to you. See how things are going."

"Last night I talked to Howard."

"You get that thing straight for him?"

"I sent Jap and Kenny to get his fifty back from the construction guy, Charles Watson, but he ducked out on them. Now he's got another problem."

"What now?"

"He said a couple of nights ago his brother was forced into the limo at gunpoint by three men. They beat him pretty bad and dumped him out of the car."

"He all right?"

"Howard says he's in the hospital, but he'll be all right. But last night somebody took a shot at him. Howard walked into the lobby of his building and somebody was waitin' there pointin' a .38. Howard ducked and the bullet grazed his right shoulder. Since he went down from the impact, the shooter thought he was dead. But Howard saw the guy get into a black Lexus. He recognized the car. Thinks it belongs to a guy that works for Watson. His name is Clay Barksdale."

"This nigga wanna play gangster?" Black laughed.

"Looks that way."

"What'd you tell him?"

"Don't worry about it. That he should go on with his business like this wasn't happenin'."

"Good." Black finished his drink and put the glass down. "Anything else I need to know about?"

"No, everything else is smooth. What do you want me to do about Charles Watson?"

"It's your house to run, handle it however you think you should. But if you're askin' for my advice, I think you should handle it personally and as violently as possible."

"Establish myself."

"Make sure people know who you are and things ain't no different. But do it in a way that leaves us an opportunity to cut into his construction company."

"I'll take care of it, but I got a question. What exactly am I establishing myself as? What I'm askin' is, are we stayin' in or am I overseeing us getting out?"

"That's entirely up to you. We're moving to be more legitimate, but as long as we're making money, I see absolutely no reason to give up that money. So what I'm tellin' you is this, it's your house to run as long as you want to and as long as you make us money."

Black looked at me for what seemed like a long time. Then he stood up and went to the bar. I thought that he was thinking about the best way for me to do what he wanted done.

"Do you remember when you used to run that crap game?" he asked while he poured.

I had no idea where he was goin' with this. "What were we, sixteen, seventeen then?"

"Something like that."

"Made a lot of money runnin' that game."

"You damn sure did. You remember Big Willie; used to always wanna fight everybody?" Black said and laughed.

"Yeah, that muthafucka was crazy," I laughed. "Talkin' 'bout killin' niggas when he lost."

"Like that night he lost all that money and said you was usin' loaded dice."

We both stopped laughing.

I hadn't thought about that night in years, but now it was like it had just happened the day before. Everybody was bettin' big money, and this kid named Ricky Wells was on a roll. Big Willie starts screamin' about how much money he lost and how the dice must be loaded.

I told him to shut the fuck up and take his broke-ass home. Then I handed the dice back to Ricky and I took my eyes off Big Willie. Before I knew it, I was on my back, and he was standing over me, pointin' a gun.

"Nobody talks to me like that!" Big Willie yelled and cocked the hammer. Just then, Black comes out of nowhere and hits Big Willie so hard that it broke his jaw.

Willie dropped the gun and grabbed his face.

Black pulled out a gun and held it to Willie's head. I didn't even know Black had a gun.

"You ain't killin' nobody tonight; especially him. Get the fuck outta here and don't ever let me catch you 'round here." Black told him that night.

I sat there nodding my head, remembering that night. "Glad you were there 'cause I was sure he was gonna kill me."

"You're like a brother to me, Nick. Just like Bobby. I wouldn't let him kill you."

"I know that."

I never knew that Black looked at me that way. I moved to the block when I was eleven. It was always him and Bobby who were like brothers. They'd been tight since the second grade. I always felt like an outsider around them. I guess I was wrong, but it felt good to know.

"Then why would you think I'd let Bobby kill you?"

Now why he wanna go there with this?

I dropped my head and buried it in the palms of my hands. I hadn't thought about that night with Big Willie, but I try not to think about that night.

Her name was Camille Augustus. She was Bobby's woman, but I was in love with her. Bobby found out and lost his mind.

I remembered it all.

"Bobby, put the gun down," Black yelled.

I felt Bobby's hand tighten around my throat.

"I'll kill you!" Bobby screamed.

Black put his gun to Bobby's head. "Bobby, please," he said quietly. "Take the gun out of his mouth and put it down."

Black moved his gun away from Bobby's head. Bobby let go of my throat and slowly eased his gun out of my mouth. I reached for my throat and took a step away from Bobby.

"Don't think this is over."

I remember walking away, trying to catch my breath; hearing Bobby screamin' "I'ma kill you. And that bitch!"

I lifted my head and Black was still looking me. I guess he was waiting for an answer. When I had none to offer, Black continued. "Why didn't you come to me?"

"The way it turned out, I should have."

Black slammed his glass down on the coffee table. "Fuck that, Nick! No matter how it turned out, you shoulda never left like you did. You shoulda came to me. I woulda settled that shit. You didn't have to join the fuckin' Army. We had just made our big move, things were 'bout to change and you're gone."

"I was wrong, Black. I know that. I thought Bobby killed Camille and would be coming for me next. You woulda been in the middle of it. I couldn't put you in that position: having to choose between me and Bobby."

"That wasn't your choice to make."

"What would you have done if Bobby shot me?"

"I don't know. I'm glad I never had to find out," Black said and I heard my cell phone ringing in the bedroom. I got up quickly and went to answer it. I was glad that it rang and hoped when I got back he would be done with it and moved on to something else.

"Hello."

"Mr. Simmons, this is Roslyn Phillips speaking. How are you today?"

"I'm doin' fine, Mrs. Phillips. How are you?"

"I'll manage. I was calling for two reasons."

"What's that, Mrs. Phillips?" I already knew what one of them was.

"I wanted to know if you had found who killed Zakiya."

"Not yet, but I'm workin' on it."

"I see. Well, I know these things take time. But I just thought I'd ask. But the main reason I was calling was to make sure that you would be at her funeral today."

I hadn't planned on going. Hadn't given it any thought at all, to be honest about it. But I promised that I would be there. Mrs. Phillips gave me the address of the church and I hung up. I went back to the living room and hoped that Black wanted to talk about Charles Watson and not me runnin' out on him.

"That was Mrs. Phillips on the phone," I said when I got back in the room.

"Wants to know about Zakiya?"

"That and whether I was comin' to her funeral."

"Are you?"

"I told her I'd be there. Since you're dressed for it, you wanna come with me?"

"No." Black said definitely. "I have a lunch meeting with Wanda and somebody else with a name I can't pronounce. After that, I gotta meet Bobby at the club to talk to P Harlem and his agent about some shit P did to lose his record deal. Then I have a dinner meeting at Cuisine with our investment banker."

"Meka Brazil?"

Black looked at me like he was surprised I knew that. Then I guess he thought about it. "Wanda."

I nodded my head.

"Tell me about Zakiya Phillips?"

"Word I got is that the shooters were Jasper Robinson's people."

"J.R.?"

"I talked to him and I don't think he knows anything about it."

"How's he doin'?"

"He looked all right to me, but his daughter says he's been sick."

"I haven't seen Lorraine and Miles since they were kids."

"She likes to be called Rain now. I didn't meet Miles yet."

"Jeff Ritchie still with him?"

"Yeah. What's his deal?"

"Jeff Ritchie is J.R.'s right hand; been with him for years."

"Why do they call him by his whole name all the time?"

"That's what J.R. always called him. I don't know why. I do know I wouldn't mind havin' J.R.'s gambling operation, but I hear Lorraine's into more than just gambling," Black said and got up to leave. "If J.R.'s involved, kill him."

Chapter 23

After Black left I hit the shower and got ready to go to Zakiya Phillips's funeral. On the way there Black's words rolled around in my mind.

Then why would you think I'd let Bobby kill you?
You shoulda came to me.

Maybe he's right. Maybe I shouldn't have left the way I did, but I wasn't about to let Bobby kill me over Camille.

I'll never forget that night. Bobby with his gun in my mouth, screamin' he was gonna kill me; Black with his gun to Bobby's head. He just kept sayin' "Bobby put the gun down." I remember lookin' at his face; his eyes. I could see the pain he was in. My two best friends. Bobby was ready to kill me. And Black, shit! I can't even imagine where his head was, with a gun to Bobby's head.

I called Camille when I left there that night to tell her what happened. She didn't care. Camille told me to come fuck her, and that was all she had to say. I was on my way, but I needed a drink first. Camille was dead when I got there. Two shots to the head. I was sure that Bobby had killed her and I was next. And I knew that if

Bobby wanted me dead, Black wouldn't have been able to stop him.

The truth was I ran out on Black when he needed me most. We had just killed André and his partner Ricky Combs. After the job, Jamaica, who at the time was strung-out on heroin, went MIA. And then I disappeared.

I thought this was over when I made peace with Bobby, but I was wrong. Me and Black would have to talk about this again; there's something I gotta say.

I arrived at the funeral just as Mrs. Phillips got out of the limo. She told me that I looked very handsome in a suit and asked me to escort her in. When we got to the first pew, she insisted that I sit next to her. She wouldn't take no for an answer.

I didn't mind.

I couldn't begin to imagine what she was feeling right now. She had raised Zakiya just like my grandmother raised me. Being with her reminded me of the times I spent with my grandmother. If my being there with her made her feel any better, I was glad to be there for her.

I don't like funerals. I've been to too many. I felt out of place sitting there. I didn't know Zakiya. I'm just the guy trying to honor an old lady's request to find who killed her granddaughter. I thought about Freeze and felt myself getting mad. I guess it showed on my face. Mrs. Phillips nudged me. "Stop looking like that," she whispered.

After the funeral, I drove away thinking about what I was gonna do next to keep my promise.

When I got to Monika's apartment, she looked surprised to see me. "I'm honored that you're here," she said when I mentioned it.

"What are you talkin' 'bout?"

"How I hear you cappo da big dog or some shit now."

"How'd you hear about it?"

"Jackie told me."

"You and Jackie ain't . . ." I had to ask.

"No. It ain't like she ain't tried me. But I like dick too much."

"What'd she say about me being boss?" It felt funny sayin' it.

"I just told you. I'm just glad to see that even though you the man now that you still got time for your old friends. But you're probably here because you need something."

"You're right, I do need something, but that don't mean I can't come see an old friend."

"So what's it like?"

"I'm gettin' used to it."

"I just never thought it was you, you know, all that gangster shit."

"What makes you say that?"

"When I met you, you were a soldier. I remember the stories you used to tell about what you used to do, and you always seemed like you were glad to put all that behind you."

"This was my life back then. Maybe this is who I really am, and I was trying to run away from it."

"Maybe. I didn't know you when this was your life. That's why it just seems funny to me."

"A lot's happened since then."

"You're right about that. 'Cause back then I never imagined I'd be doin' what I'm doin'."

"You have any luck with those e-mails?"

"Of course I did. Like I told you, I may not be as good as Jett, but I have skills too. This was easy, I got something goin' and I sure could use his help."

"What you workin' on?" I asked, but she didn't answer me and gave me one of her looks. Whatever she was into she didn't want to tell me. I respected her privacy. We talked for awhile after that and I got out of there. What I got from Monika came as a bit of a surprise, but it shouldn't have. The pieces were starting to fit together.

Monika told me that the e-mails were sent from a computer at J.R.'s club. What she couldn't tell me was who the account holder was, or more to the point, what their real name was.

"It was set up last October with the first name, Nice; middle name, N; and the last name, Slow," Monika told me.

When I got to J.R.'s it was early in the evening. They didn't have much of a crowd yet. It gave me a chance to talk to the staff and show them the picture I took from Zakiya's apartment.

I had shown it to a few people before I found one who thought she recognized her. "Yeah," the waitress said and looked at the picture a little closer. "I seen her before. This picture was taken here," she said and pointed to the spot where Zakiya posed for the picture. She called over one of her co-workers. She looked at the picture; she had seen Zakiya there too. "Yup, she be up in here all the time."

"You ever see her with anybody?" I asked as Jeff Ritchie came into the club. He stopped in his tracks when he saw me.

"I don't remember her being with nobody, but she be in here all the time."

I looked at Jeff Ritchie again; he turned away and went in the back of the club. It couldn't have been two minutes later when Rain came out of the back and headed in my direction.

She was wearing a purple mini-skirt that showed off some very pretty legs, and a white silk blouse that was tied just under a healthy set of titties. As she got closer, I wondered where she was hiding her gun.

When the waitresses saw Rain coming, they dropped their heads and left me standing there to face her alone.

I smiled when I saw the *what the fuck are you doin' here* look on her face. The question now was how was I gonna play Rain? Since she played me, it was only fair that I returned the favor.

Since the e-mails were sent from somewhere in this building, I assumed that whoever this Nice N. Slow was that they worked here, or had access to whatever computers they had. The question for me was does Rain know who it is.

I think she does.

If that was the case, I know she had to be thinking that she had gotten rid of me with her bullshit and I would look someplace else for Zakiya's killers.

If she didn't it would make things more interesting.

"Couldn't stay away from me?" Rain said when she got close enough for me to hear her over the music.

"That's one way of lookin' at it."

"Whatever it is, Nick, I'm glad to see you. Maybe this time you'll have a drink with me."

"That's what I'm here for."

"What you drinkin'?"

"Johnnie Black, straight up."

Rain signed for one of the waitresses I had just talked to. She tried not to even look in my direction. Rain told her what I wanted. "And bring me a shot of Patron."

After the waitress went to get our drinks, Rain turned back to me. "You find your shooters yet?"

"Not yet. But I heard from some of her friends that she liked to hangout here." I took out the picture. "I got a picture of her," I said and handed Rain the picture. I was anxious to see the expression on her face and the look in her eye when she saw Zakiya's picture, but there was none.

"Never seen her before. You show that to anybody else here, maybe one of the waitresses seen her here."

"I did but nobody recognized her," I lied.

"I ain't surprised. A lotta people come through here every night."

"It was a shot in the dark."

"You were just lookin' for an excuse to come see me, that's all."

"That's one way of lookin' at it." The waitress came back with our drinks and disappeared quickly. "I was hopin' that you would show me around your spot, maybe play a couple of hands of poker." I needed to have a look around for computers. That would give me a better idea of who had access to them. I don't remember seeing one in J.R.'s office, but I wasn't actually looking for one that night. I knew there had to be at least one.

I told Rain that I wanted to play poker because Black said he wouldn't mind takin' over J.R.'s gambling operation.

"Not a problem," Rain said and stood up. I followed her, watching how her wide hips swung in the mini as she showed me around the club.

We had been all through the club and I hadn't seen a single computer anywhere. Then we went in the back. Rain showed me the dressing rooms for the entertainment and the door to gambling room.

"We'll go down there in a minute."

The next door we came to was locked, so Rain knocked. "That door always locked?" I asked.

"Most of the time. This is Miles's office."

"That's your brother, right?"

"Right." A woman came to the door. "I'm not interrupting, am I?" Rain asked and walked by the woman.

"How are you doin'?" I said to the woman and followed Rain in.

There was a computer on the desk.

"What's up, Miles? There's somebody I want you to meet." Miles stood up and came from behind his desk.

"I'm Miles Robinson," he said and extended his hand. By that time the woman who opened the door was standing next to Miles. "And this is my wife, Lakeda."

"Nick Simmons."

Miles looked impressed. "It's good to meet you. Heard a lot about you."

"I was about to take Nick downstairs, but I wanted to introduce y'all before I went down there. You know how you like to run outta here. I'm surprised you're still here," Rain said and turned to leave. "Oh, by the way," she turned to me. "Show them the picture, Nick."

"Y'all ever see this girl up in here?" Rain asked as I handed Miles the picture. He looked at the picture and handed it back to me.

"No, I haven't."

"I didn't think you would. Just thought I'd ask," Rain said and headed for the door.

I looked at Miles and then at Lakeda.

"You comin'?" Rain said.

"Nice meeting you both."

Chapter 24

Mike Black

My dinner meeting with Meka Brazil turned into dinner with Meka and Wanda. When Meka mentioned that she was meeting me for dinner, Wanda invited herself to join us; which turned out to be a good thing 'cause she told me that State Senator Martin Marshall was having a fundraiser that night, and Mr. Marshall was somebody I needed to have a conversation with.

Wanda's presence at dinner with Meka did put an entirely different spin on the night. Especially when Meka looked at her watch and announced she was late for that evening's conference call. She immediately slapped her Bluetooth on her ear, started punching numbers on her Blackberry, apologized and ran out of there.

Wanda turned to me. "That's gonna be you one day."

"No. It's not. I can't ever imagine a time when I'll become as attached to that thing as she is. I don't have a cell phone. I don't like bein' that accessible."

"You're already accessible. You're on Kevon's phone more than he is," Wanda said.

"That's because you, Meka, and now Bobby call me all

the time to talk about what we just talked about at the meeting."

"Which reminds me, how did your meeting go with P Harlem?"

"How does any meetin' with P go? P talked, we listened."

Paul 'P Harlem' Roberts is one of the two major rapper clients that Wanda represents. The other is The One. His real name is Earl, real nice guy. Get that nigga a bag of weed and some pussy and he's a happy man. But not P. Don't get me wrong, he's all for pussy and weed. P is words, P is conscience, P is anger. That's what his music is all about. But he's real about it, so he says what he thinks. Sometimes it gets him in trouble.

There was an incident at strip club in Atlanta, P was there with his whole set and they're droppin' paper like its water. Some young gangster comes in, sees P, and gets the DJ to put him on the mic. When he gets done, he comes over to P and says, "What you think?"

P says, "Somebody got to explain to me why they even let you near the mic with that weak shit," and turns his back on the little gangster.

Shots were fired and the little gangster ends up dead. P was arrested but the case was thrown out. There were no witnesses. People could definitely say that P was there that night, but nobody saw him with a gun. "But that ain't his problem this time."

"What is it now?"

"He won some award, so at the show P gets up and says he'd like to thank his record company, 'But I can't 'cause they robbed me blind. These bitches want me to sing and dance, but they want me to do it for free.' Now they won't re-sign him."

"I know all about it. But that's not why they don't want to sign him," Wanda said.

"Why not?"

"There's only so much of a market for what Paul does. They told him if he started callin' women bitches and hoes that he'd sell more records."

"What about them robbin' him blind? Isn't that, like, our job to see that they don't rob him blind?"

"All legitimate expenses incurred by Paul. The contract allowed them to subtract tour expenses from his royalties."

"I understand now. But don't you usually send somebody on tour with them to keep shit like this from happening?"

"I did. I sent Webster Houston."

"What happened?"

"He said he was seduced by the dark side of the force," Wanda said and shook her head.

"P turned him out?"

"Something about how orgies and room service go together." Wanda looked disgusted. "So what did he want?"

"He just wanted to vent." Actually he wanted me to kill some A&R guy at the record company for disrespecting him. I told him that I wouldn't kill him, but he should expect an apology.

But Wanda didn't need to know about all that.

I've been making a real effort to keep her away from that side of things. I've been thinking that it's not a good idea for her to be the managing partner of our legitimate businesses and be advising a criminal organization. Better she stick to business.

What surprised me is how Bobby has gotten into the whole legit thing. Bobby always has looked at things a little differently from the rest of us. So he asks Meka a lot of questions—makes her explain shit. I don't think she likes Bobby. But he gets me to see things in ways that I hadn't considered.

"How'd you leave it with him?" Wanda asked.

"I told him that I'd think about starting a record company."

Wanda looked at me without speaking while she considered the possibilities. "That could work for us."

"See what it's gonna take to make that happen and get back to me," I told Wanda. Then I looked up and saw something that I never thought I'd see.

There in the foyer stood Angelo Collette and two of his men. Angelo was giving my manager Lexi a hard time, and pointing at me. She's probably tellin' him that she don't care who he says he knows, he's not getting in without a reservation.

I looked at Kevon, he was looking at me. I nodded my head; Kevon went to take care of it. That's another reason why I chose him to be my bodyguard, Kevon never misses anything. He's always aware of his environment and he's always looking around so he sees everything.

"Isn't that Angelo at the door?" Wanda said when she noticed the commotion.

"Yeah." I watched as Kevon settled Lexi down and then let Angelo pass. He escorted Angelo's men to the bar.

"What's he doing here?"

"I don't know. I've been trying to get Angee to come here for years. He wants something. Something major or he wouldn't be here." Probably some Crazy Joe shit. Out of respect, I stood up to greet him. Wanda did too.

"Mikey, Wanda," Angelo said and shook my hand. "How's everybody doing tonight?" Angelo hugged Wanda and kissed her on the cheek.

"I'm fine, Angelo."

"How long has it been since I saw you, Wanda?" Angelo asked and took a seat.

"Been at least eight years."

"Well, you're as beautiful as I remember."

I sat down without speaking and listened while Wanda

and Angee made small talk like two old friends that hadn't seen each other in years. While they talked, I couldn't help but wonder what would make Angee come up here. It's rare when he leaves his little area in Yonkers.

"Wanda, I don't mean to be rude, but I need to talk to this guy."

Wanda stood up, so did Angelo. "I didn't think you came here just to tell me how pretty I was. It was good seeing you."

"Great seeing you, too."

"We should talk more when you have some time," Wanda said and looked at me. She wanted to explore, as she called it, legitimate business opportunities with Angee, but she knows I'm against it. Angee has his own problems with the law. This is not the time to be in business with him. But Wanda can be hard-headed sometimes. She turned to me. "I'll be in the office, Mike."

Wanda said goodnight to Angee and headed for the office. As soon as she walked off, Angelo leaned toward me and whispered. "Can we talk in here?"

"I have the place swept for bugs every day. But we can talk outside if it makes you more comfortable."

I stood up and led Angee out the back door. Kevon and Angee's men followed behind us.

Once we had gotten a little ways down the street, Angee got to the purpose of his visit. "I wanted to ask you about Stark."

I wasn't expecting that. "What about him?"

"I hear he's a serious man, who's deserving of respect."

Now I knew what Angee wanted. He hasn't been a player in this game since Cassandra got out. She had a dual degree in management and marketing, saw drug dealing as a business, and ran her program that way.

I learned a lot about business from her. One more reason to miss her. With the direction we're taking now, Cassandra's advice and involvement would have been invaluable to me.

When she left the country with me, Chilly sucked up what was left of her operation. With the rest of his Commission dead or in the wind, Stark controlled a big chunk of the drug market and Angee wanted back in. "You want to meet him?"

"I was hopin' for something a little more than just an introduction from you, Mikey."

"Like what?"

"I was thinkin' that maybe you would take more of an active role. You could be kind of a stabilizing influence. You know, keep problems down."

"What makes you think I got that kind of influence with Stark?"

"Come on, Mikey. You're a legend 'round here. Stark probably grew up hearing stories about you. I hear this kid respects you; idolizes you. And I also hear that you like him."

"You hear a lot of things."

"I do."

Definitely wasn't expecting this.

"I know I'm asking a lot of you. I know you're tryin' to move in a different direction. But with Stark out front you wouldn't have to get your hands dirty. Naturally, you could charge a fee for your influence." Then he hit me with it. "I would consider it a personal favor."

Definitely wasn't expecting this.

"You are askin' a lot." I stopped walking and looked Angee in the eye. "I'll tell you what I will do. I'll set up a meeting with you and Stark. I have to think about what you just asked me, for personal reasons."

"I understand completely, Mikey. All I can ask is that you think about it."

Chapter 25

"What him want, boss?" Kevon wanted to know as we watched Angee drive off.

"Something I don't wanna do," I said and started walking toward the club.

I definitely wasn't expecting Angee to come outta nowhere with that shit. I should have told him no. I should have said, flat out, no. What you ask, I can not do. I should have said that I can't do it for personal reasons that he is well aware of, and that I was insulted that he would ask.

But I didn't.

I've been goin' to Angee with my problems for years, and he never, not once, has asked anything in return—until now. As Kevon drove, I thought about what my refusing Angee might cost me.

On the way to Marshall's fundraiser with Wanda I didn't have much to say. She asked me what Angee wanted, but I gave her the same answer I gave Kevon. When she pushed it, I told her that Angee wanted to talk about Crazy Joe and to my surprise, she left it alone.

Crazy Joe Delfino used to do jobs with Angelo back in the day. Me, him, and Angelo were supposed to hijack a load of cigarettes. But me and Angee got there late, so Crazy Joe did the job alone. He was arrested by Newark police at the tollbooth when he got off the turnpike.

Joe found out later that we were late because on the way to the job, we stopped to rob a jewelry store to settle an argument.

The robbery went off without any problems, but we got stuck in traffic coming across the George Washington Bridge. When we got there we found Crazy Joe's car, but no Joe. Angelo found out the next day that Joe was arrested. Since then he's been talkin' 'bout killin' me. He says it was my fault that he got arrested. It ain't my fault that he went and did the shit by himself. He should have waited for us. That shit didn't make no fuckin' sense. But they don't call him Crazy Joe for nothing.

We arrived at the fundraiser in time to catch the speeches. Marshall spoke last. Martin Marshall was a state senator who I'd done business with a few times. But he was such a greedy fuck that I had to cut him loose years ago. Since we had no business ties, when Glynnis told me he was involved in Cassandra's murder, I wanted to kill him. But I knew that he would be more useful alive. Without Martin's help, DeFrancisco might still be alive.

Now he was running for congress, and if you can believe the polls, he's probably gonna win. It was good business for me to re-establish our association.

After his speech, Martin made his way around the room, shaking hands and nodding his head as people told him their problems or asked him for favors. When Martin first saw me I could tell that he was surprised to see me standing there, maybe a little scared. But he very quickly separated himself from the people he was talking to and made his way to me.

"Good evening, Mr. Black," Martin said and shook my hand. "I am more than surprised to see you here." He turned to Wanda. "How are you, Wanda?" She was no stranger to these events. "How did you ever get this guy out to a stuffy event like this?"

"All it took was the mention of your name," Wanda said 'cause it was true. Martin's involvement with DeFrancisco made him my best source of information about Pete Vinnelli. That and the fact that if he is elected, having Martin tucked away in my pocket just made sense.

"Is that a fact?" Martin said and leaned close to me. "There's a place we can talk upstairs," he said and walked off.

"I'll be back," I said to Wanda and followed Martin to the elevator. Neither of us spoke in the elevator or in the hallway as Martin led me to a room. Once inside, Martin took a small device out of his pocket and set it on the desk.

"What's that?"

"Everybody's listening these days. This puts out just enough of a signal to make whatever they do pick up too distorted to be admissible in court."

"I should get one of those."

"Yes. Now tell me what I can do for you? Actually, I'm not all that surprised to see you. I heard you were making a move to the other side of the street."

"You heard that, huh?"

"If that's true, we could be very valuable to one another."

"Yes, we could. But I don't know that I could trust you, Martin."

"Yes. That unfortunate business about your wife."

If I had my gun it would be at the base of his skull right now. Martin always was an arrogant fuck, but he wasn't stupid. "I thought we'd settled that between us."

"That was just a down payment."

"Tell me how we call it even."

"Pete Vinnelli. I want him. And you're gonna give him to me."

I looked at Martin and wondered why he was smiling. "He's yours."

"What are you smiling about?" I demanded to know. Damn he's annoying.

"I've been expecting you."

"Really?" Now I'm predicable.

"The last time we talked; you remember, you and Bobby forced your way into my house and held guns on me?"

"I remember, Martin."

"I wasn't expecting you. I didn't see any way that you could possibly connect me with DeFrancisco and Estaban. I underestimated you. It's a mistake I will never make again. But there you were, with every reason in the world to kill me, but you wanted DeFrancisco, and I gave him to you. To make a long story short, I knew you'd be back one day and you would want Vinnelli."

"You're right. But I'm not the only one that wants him, am I? Vinnelli can link you to DeFrancisco. You want him—no, that's not strong enough. You need Vinnelli dealt with."

"Something you want for something I need. That makes us partners."

"I think that's taking it a little far."

"Then we'll call it two mutually interested parties."

"However you want to look at it, the problem is how do you kill a DEA agent without attracting attention."

Martin looked at me. "I'll just say some people have been very lucky in that regard and leave it at that."

"Some people have all the luck." From that, I knew he knew that I was responsible for the recent deaths of agents Masters and Harris.

Martin moved a little closer to me and spoke a little lower. "Here's what I can give you. For some time now you've had a very talented hacker digging around in Vinnelli's finances, but there is one piece that continues to elude them."

"How do you know that, Martin?"

"Believe me, Mr. Black; I know a great deal about a great many things. Like I said, I've been expecting you, so I know what I need to know."

"What's that?"

"Eileen McManus."

"Who is that?"

"She is everything you need, Mr. Black," Martin said. "That should make us even," he said and extended his hand. I accepted his hand. "When you're finished with this matter we'll talk again about what we can do for each other in the future."

As I rode the elevator down with Martin, one thing hit me. This wasn't the same Martin Marshall I'd dealt with years ago. I realized then that I was about to start playing in whole new world. In that world, Martin Marshall was already a player. I would have to be very careful in my dealings with him.

The fact that he was expecting me and knew exactly what I wanted didn't bother me. He needs Vinnelli out of the way, but he doesn't want to get his hands dirty with an election coming, so he serves him up to me. That's fine. I was willing to be used if it got me Vinnelli. But what does bother me is what happens after that.

I've been expecting you.

That meant Martin had plans for me.

Chapter 26

Nick

I looked back at Miles and Lakeda and then followed Rain to the gambling room. She entered the combination to the door and we went down a long flight of stairs. "He's with me," she told the two men standing by the door. One got up to open it for her.

"You are so sweet." Rain touched his face as she passed. I followed her into a large room with four tables in each corner of the room; one for poker and one for blackjack. There was one table where a lively crap game was goin' on, and people held their breath for each turn of the roulette wheel. There in the middle of it all was Jeff Ritchie sitting in what I'm sure used to be J.R.'s spot.

If J.R. was involved in this and I had to kill him, Jeff Ritchie would have to die first. I looked around the room and tried to get a feel for what kind of muscle he had. My eyes met his and he glared at me. I could tell that he didn't like me hangin' around there. I'm sure he knows what I represent. I nodded my head to acknowledge him and smiled. *"Yeah, mutha fucka, I'm gonna kill you and take over this spot,"* I said to myself and waved to him as Rain slid in next to me and handed me another drink.

"What you think?"

"Impressive."

"Wait here and I'll see if I can't get you a seat at the table," Rain said and left me alone.

I wandered around the room looking over Jeff Ritchie's men, wondering if one of them was Nice N. Slow, or if it was Miles. He is married and the only computer in the building is in his office, so it does make him the logical choice. There was the possibility that somebody else, Jeff Ritchie maybe, could have a key to Miles's office.

I stood and watched as Rain went straight to Jeff Ritchie to get me in the game. I knew from that, that Rain carried no weight down here.

I walked around and stood by the poker table and thought back to Miles's expression when I showed them Zakiya's picture. He glanced at the picture quickly like he was trying not to look at it.

What was more interesting was when I looked back and saw the expression on Lakeda's face. The way she was looking at Miles made me believe that he was Nice N. Slow and she knew, or at least suspected, he was cheating on her. I needed to get a picture of Miles and show it to Tasheka and Shameka at Paradise. And even if it is Miles, that didn't mean that he killed her.

"We can buy in on the next hand," Rain said, suddenly appearing next to me.

"We? You play?"

"I hold my own."

After we played a few hands of poker we left the gambling room and went back upstairs. "Well, what you think?"

"Like I said, I'm impressed. Looks like y'all run a smooth little operation here."

"But it's nothin' compared to y'all's, right?"

"I don't know. What else you got?"

"What you mean?"

"I mean is this all you got?"

"No, we got a few other spots that do pretty good for us."

"But nothing like this, right? This is y'all's big spot."

Rain put her hands on her hips. "So what you sayin'? That this ain't shit?"

"I ain't sayin' shit. You the one tryin' to make the comparison."

"Come on, nigga. Let me show you how we roll," Rain said and grabbed me by the hand.

Thank you, I thought as we fought our way through the crowded club. I was starting to think she wasn't gonna take the bait.

Rain led me to her car and we drove off. She took me to around to four of their spots and bragged about having five more. "But they too far and I don't feel like ridin' out there," Rain told me and took me back to J.R.'s. I really was impressed with what I saw.

The reception Rain got at the spots we went to was different than it was at J.R.'s. Everywhere we went, it was obvious that she was the queen and everybody bowed down to her. More importantly, every place we went was makin' money.

When we got back to J.R.'s, Rain led me back to the offices. "This is Pops' office."

"Where's yours?"

"I don't have one. Don't need one."

J.R. wasn't there that night, but she had a key to his office. We went in the office and Rain picked up the remote for the flat screen. "Pops is rarely here at night these days, so when he's not here this is my spot." She dropped the remote and headed for the bar. "Johnnie Black, right?"

"Right," I said and looked at the flat screen. Porn star Lola Lane appeared on the screen, ridin' some guy's dick, talkin' 'bout, *'Yeah, Lola likes that. Fuck Lola's pussy.'*

I looked at Rain, she looked at me. "Ooops," she said and pushed a button on the bar and the image on the screen changed. Now the screen displayed images from around the club. "Sorry about that."

I sat down on whatever seat was closest to me without commenting on Lola or Rain's apology. I looked around the office and my eyes stopped on a picture of a much younger J.R. and a very pretty woman.

Rain handed me my drink and sat down. "Is that your mother in that picture," I said and pointed to it.

"Yup, that's my mom, Barbara Robinson."

"She's very pretty," I said and thought that Miles looked a lot like her.

"She was beautiful. She died when I was a baby, so I never really knew her."

"For some reason I thought you were older than Miles."

"Most people think that. But he's older by eleven months."

"You and him must be close."

"We used to be."

"What changed that?"

"Why you wanna know?"

I laughed. "Why you gettin' defensive?"

"I'm not. We just ain't close like we used to be."

"That got anything to do with your sister-in-law?"

"You ask a lot of fuckin' questions," Rain said and finished her drink.

"I just noticed that you two didn't really speak to each other."

Rain got up and headed toward the bar. "I don't like the bitch. Never have. I haven't spoken to her since I was in the seventh grade. There. You happy now?"

"Why don't you make me one too?" I said and finished my drink. "Why don't you like her? She seems like a nice person."

"Yeah, yeah, she's real nice and whatever. I just don't like her, and let's leave it at that." When Rain came back she had both bottles. Like she planned on us being there for a while. That was fine with me. I had a lot of questions for her; about her brother and their operation. Specifically; what else she had going on. If we do move on them, I wanted there to be as few surprises as possible.

She took my glass and poured me a drink. As soon as she poured herself a shot, I raised my glass.

"Didn't mean to make you mad," I said and drained my glass. Rain followed suit and drained hers.

I took the glass from her hand and poured her another and one for myself.

"I would rather drink to something else," Rain said.

"What do you wanna drink to?"

Rain raised her glass. "Anything that don't have nothin' to do with Lakeda Johnson." Rain turned up her glass. "Talk to me about something else."

"Like what?"

"I don't know; anything."

"I'd rather talk about you."

"Why you wanna know about me?"

"You already know 'bout me. Only thing I know about you is that you're twenty-two. I know you can handle a gun."

Rain looked at me and smiled. I was starting to like the way she smiled. Rain had those pouty lips I seem to like so much. "My daddy taught me how to shoot."

"You daddy's little girl?"

"Yup. Everything I know that's important I learned from him. He taught me a lot about dealin' with people."

"How to get them to do what you want them to do?"

"That too. But he taught me to look and listen. Said that's why we got two eyes and two ears."

"And only one mouth."

"Exactly." Rain poured herself another drink. "I remember once when I was in high school."

"What school did you go to?"

"Immaculate Conception."

"Catholic school girl."

"And I ain't even catholic. Pops sent me there after I got kicked out of public school . . ."

"What you get kicked out for?"

"Fightin'. Let this mouth get me into somethin' I had to fight my way out of. That's when he told me about lookin' and listenin' to mugs, see where they really coming from. But when I first got there these girls wanted to try me, you know, 'cause I'm new and shit. But I just got kicked out of school for fightin', so I'm tryin' to be cool. But these bitches won't let up. So I tell Pops about it."

"What he say?"

"He listened, and then he said, 'I can't tell you what to do. I could tell you what I would do if I was in your place.' Then he said that I had to start makin' my own decisions, and once I made those decisions that I had to be willing to stand up and be responsible for those decisions."

"Good advice."

"Yeah, I've lived by it since. But anyway, he said this is a matter of honor. You already know what the right thing to do is. The right thing is not to fight in school. So if it's just a question of right and wrong, the choice was easy."

"Don't fight in school."

"That was the right thing. He said what I have to decided is if doin' the right shit worth what I had to give up?"

"Your honor."

"Pops told me once that all you really have at the end of the day is your honor. If you don't have honor you don't have shit. I know the right thing was to let them bitch-punk me everyday, tell a teacher or some shit. I tried all that, it didn't work. I had to beat the bitch down, but it was a decision I had to make for myself."

"What you do?"

"They would always come at me in the lunchroom. So, like, I'm in line, right, gettin' my food and here they come."

"How many?"

"Four. Soon as this bitch says something to me, I takes my tray and wheeled around on her ass. I caught her in the face with it and she starts cryin' like a fuckin' baby. After all that tough talk, this bitch is cryin' like a baby. You believe that shit?"

"Sometimes bullies are all talk."

"Yeah, no shit. I just kept hittin' her with that tray until the teachers came and pulled me off her ass. The other kids was cheerin' and shit, 'get her, get her,' 'cause this bitch used to fuck with everybody. Nobody liked her, but they was all afraid of her. I got a rush from beatin' her ass. It was the best feelin'."

"Did they kick you out?"

"Pops had paid for the year in advance and he spread some money around, so they just suspended me since everybody knew she had been fuckin' with me since I got there."

"I bet nobody fucked with you when you got back?"

"Nope. I was the queen fuckin' bee after that."

I raised my glass. "To the queen."

Rain raised her glass and pointed at me. "Queen needs a king."

For the next couple of hours I sat in the office drinking shots with Rain while she flirted with me and I asked her questions. The more Patron she drank, the easier it was to get answers. I needed to know about their gambling operations, and what exactly she was in to, but I worked it into conversation so it didn't seem like I was interrogating her.

When Rain announced, "I'm fucked up in this bitch." I finished my drink and stood up.

"Where you goin'?" Rain said and tried to get up, but couldn't.

"I got something to do."

"Why you gotta go?" she pouted. "Have another drink with me."

"You don't need no more to drink and besides, you haven't even finished the one you got."

"Oh yeah," Rain said and looked at the glass in her hand. She put the glass down and tried again to get up. I held out my hand to help her up. "Thank you," she said in a whisper. "You can't go."

"Yes, I can."

Rain took a step closer. "So you think you can just come in here, get my ass drunk, ask me a bunch-of-fuckin' questions, and then leave?"

"Yes, I do."

"No, Nick. That's not right. You can't leave me like this."

"This is your spot; you'll be all right here."

Rain took a step closer but she stumbled a little. I caught her before she fell. She pressed her body against mine and put her arms around me. "That ain't what I mean. You can't leave me like this. The least you could do is drive me home, strip me down and put my ass to bed so I can sleep this off, 'cause, I'm for real, I'm fucked up," Rain laughed and so did I.

What was I supposed to do?

"Come on, Rain." I stepped away and took her by the hand. "Can you walk?"

"Long as you don't let me fall I can walk."

Rain showed me the way out the back door. That's when I saw it, another computer sitting on a desk where anybody and everybody could use it.

We made it to my car without her doin' too much stumbling. I unlocked the door and helped her get in. When I started the car I turned to Rain. Her eyes were closed. "Where do you live?"

"Mount Vernon," she said and repositioned herself.

"Where?" I asked and turned on the navigation system. Rain said the address and made herself comfortable.

Rain slept through the drive to her apartment. While she slept, I thought about what I was doing, and more importantly, what I was about to do. I mean its not like I don't see where this was goin'.

Rain had been flirting with me all night and I went along with it because I wanted something. I could have shut it down anytime I wanted to, but I didn't. I used it. Used her.

I had sized-up her father's gambling operation and she told me everything I needed to know about her brother. But now I wasn't so sure that it was Miles. Anybody could have sent those e-mails. I was back to square one.

But either way, I got what I came for, so what was I still doing with her? Drunk or not, I could have left Rain right where she was, and she would be just fine.

I thought about Wanda. I loved her, but I had to admit that Rain moved me in ways Wanda doesn't. They were exact opposites. Wanda's a businesswoman and Rain's a ride-or-die chick.

"Rain, Rain." I nudged her. "We're here."

The ride seemed to have sobered Rain up enough that

she got out of the car under her own power. "I'm okay, I can walk," she slurred as she gathered herself together. I was thankful. Carrying her inside was the last thing I wanted to do.

Rain semi-staggered toward her door and fumbled for her keys. Once she unlocked the door I started to say goodnight. "I'll—"

She grabbed me by the arm.

"Come in, I want to show you my place."

"Just for a minute, I got someplace I need to be."

"Have a seat," she said, stepping out of her heels as soon as she walked through the door. I followed her in, looking around the apartment. "Very nice, Rain."

"Thank you," she said and started walking toward the back of the apartment.

I started to sit on the couch, but selected a lone chair instead. "You want a drink?" she said when she came back.

"What do you have?" From where I was seated it looked like she had taken off her bra.

"Patron okay? It'll have to be, it's all I have."

"I guess it will have to be," I stood up and walked toward the kitchen. Rain came out carrying the bottle and two glasses. She handed me a glass and then took a step closer. "What should we drink to?"

"I don't know," I replied, stepping toward Rain almost out of instinct.

"Let's drink to tonight. I had a good time with you."

"I enjoyed you too. We have to hangout again."

"Do you mean that?" Rain said, almost in disbelief. "You wanna hangout with me?"

"Yeah."

"I was startin' to think you didn't like me."

"Why? Because I'm not all over you?"

"Yes. Most men can't resist me, but you treat me like a little girl."

We toasted our night and emptied our glasses. I leaned forward to put my glass on the bar just as Rain reached for the bottle to refill the glasses. Her breasts brushed softly against my chest, ending all speculation about the bra.

Rain handed me my glass and stepped to my chest again. She exhaled. I felt her nipples brush my chest. My eyes met hers then dropped to her cleavage. She followed my eyes. Rain touched my face and she kissed me. It caught me off guard at first, but slowly I warmed to the task and put my body into that kiss.

I thought about Wanda, thought about what I was about to do and pulled up. When I stepped away from Rain I saw somebody at her window, and then I saw the gun.

I grabbed Rain by the shoulders and pushed her down behind the couch. We stared into each other eyes while the bullets flew over us.

"I want to fuck you so bad," Rain said.

When the shooting stopped Rain jumped up and ran toward the front door. She grabbed a gun from the lamp table by the door and ran out. I ran out after her. I got outside in time to see two men running down the street. Rain began firing wildly in their direction while she ran.

A Chrysler 300 stopped in front of them and they started to get in. I fired and hit one of them before he made it in. The other one got in the car and they drove off and left him there. Rain kept running behind the car, busting shots the whole time.

I went for the car and caught up with Rain. I pulled up alongside of her. "Get in!" I yelled and took off after the 300. It turned the corner and sped away.

Rain let down the window and fired again. "I'm empty." I handed her mine. "Do you see them?"

"Over there, on your right. About two cars ahead," I answered as I weaved in and out of traffic until I caught up. The 300 turned sharp onto Lincoln Avenue. As they crossed Columbus the light turned yellow.

"Don't lose him," Rain yelled.

"I won't." I stepped on it and just barely made it before the light turned red. Just then, the 300 cut across lanes, causing the cars to crash in front of me.

"Shit!"

I slammed on my brakes, turned sharply to the left to get around it, then I had to swerve to the right to avoid the on-coming cars.

As I got closer, Rain started shooting. This time she hit the left rear tire. The 300 spun out of control and slammed into some parked cars. I pulled over ahead of the wrecked 300. With guns drawn, Rain and I approached the car slowly. There were two men in the car. Both of them appeared to be alive. I recognized them as I got closer. They were with Shake the night Rain shot him.

"You niggas?" Rain raised her gun and started shooting through the window. I emptied my clip. We stood there looking at each other for awhile before we went back to my car.

Chapter 27

When we got back to Rain's apartment the cops were there, so we decided not to stay. "I need some place to stay," Rain said as we drove away. I stopped at the first motel I got to. I left Rain in the car and went to get a room for her. "You okay?"

"I'm good."

She was quiet, uncharacteristically quiet, after what we had just been through. The last time there was gunplay involved in our evening, Rain was on fire. But not this time; this time Rain was meek, almost innocent acting, and I wondered why?

Once I had the key, I went to get Rain from the car, but she wasn't there. I looked around and saw her standing a little ways down the street.

I took my time walking to her. I figured she needed some space or time to think, or maybe she just needed some air. I don't know which it was, but I was determined to let her have it.

Rain's back was turned so she didn't see me coming and was startled when I touched her shoulder.

"You okay?" I asked again.

Rain turned around quickly. "Yeah," she said and started walking back toward the motel.

Once we got to the room and went inside, Rain tossed her purse on the bed and was all over me. She kissed me a few times and began fumbling with my belt. This time I didn't pull up.

I didn't want to.

I wanted her.

I wasn't exactly sure why, for the moment I didn't care. I ripped her blouse open and squeezed her breasts until Rain got my pants undone and dropped to her knees.

I took off my shirt and looked down as Rain slid her lips across every inch of it. Then she took me into her mouth. My excitement intensified as I watched my dick going in and out of her mouth.

Rain lifted her skirt a little and began massaging her clit. When she moaned from the pleasure she was giving herself, I took the opportunity to pull her up by her shoulders. Her body was beautiful. Rain threw her arms around me and kissed me before turning and leaning over the bed. She reached for her purse and pulled out a three-pack of condoms.

I stepped out of my pants and fell in behind her. I ran my hands over her ass and then up and down her back. Rain's body shook a little when I ran one finger down from her ass, along her lips to her clit. Rain moaned, "What are you waiting for?" I put on a condom, spread her lips, and pushed myself inside her; Rain moaned louder. "Oooh, yeah. Fuck me!"

I leaned forward, grabbed Rain by the shoulders, and began slamming myself in and out of her. When I let go of her hips Rain began grinding herself back at me, furiously pounding that juicy ass into me until her body started to tremble. "Ooooooooh!" I grabbed one of her cheeks and squeezed it as Rain began to buck harder and harder and I smacked her ass. I reached between her legs, fingering her clit with one hand and squeezing her breast with the other.

I closed my eyes and saw Wanda's face. I quickly opened them and pushed the image out of my mind.

Rain screamed and moved away from me. She rolled over on her back and lifted her legs. "Come get this pussy."

When I got up on the bed, Rain sat up and took me into her mouth again. I laid down on the bed. She began kissing me passionately and stroking my erection; her hands were all over my body. I closed my eyes and lost myself in the sensation of hands and lips against my chest and then down to my throbbing erection. I watched her head move up and down quickly.

Rain got on top of me, grabbed her hips, and slowly slid down on me. With her eyes squeezed tightly shut, Rain rode me slowly; grinding her hips until I was so deep inside her that her body started to tremble. "Damn, this dick is so fuckin' good."

Rain's words excited me; I arched my back and pushed myself as deep and as hard as I could into her. The force knocked Rain forward and she collapsed on my chest. Rain shoved her tongue in my mouth and kept her ass moving. I kissed her until she sat straight up and I took a nipple into my mouth.

Rain grabbed the back of my head and I licked and sucked her nipples and continued to push myself inside her. Her head drifted back, her eyes opened wide; she screamed and slipped off me.

Rain rolled on her back and I eased myself inside her. I began a steady motion and Rain wrapped her legs

around my waist. Rain worked her hips and inner-
muscles while licking my nipples. Now it was me whose
body began to tremble and Rain who was pounding her
hips furiously. My body went rigid and I exploded inside her.

Chapter 28

Mike Black

"Where to, boss?" Kevon asked me after we dropped Wanda off.

"Get Bobby on the phone. Find out where he is and take me to him."

Wanda wasn't happy when she got out the car, and to be honest, if it was me I'd be feeling the same way. I knew she didn't like me closing her out, but she understands. So she didn't push it too hard when I made up that bullshit about Crazy Joe.

"I know Angelo didn't leave his hole just to talk about Crazy Joe, but I'll leave it alone."

But when I excluded her from the meeting with Martin and then wouldn't tell her what we talked about, she lost her mind.

"What do you mean you didn't talk about anything in particular? The two of you were sure gone a long time for just small talk."

"It didn't seem that long to me."

"Mike, I understand you keeping me out of the loop with Angelo, but Martin is another matter. Unless you're telling me otherwise, then Martin Marshall is a legitimate business contact and I should have been there with you."

As far as Wanda knew, we hadn't had business in years. She doesn't know that Martin and I have some fresh history. I never told her that Martin had any involvement in or knowledge of Cassandra's death. I intended to keep it way.

"Bobby is at the club, boss," Kevon informed me and headed in that direction.

"Let me see the phone." Kevon handed me the phone and I dialed Monika's number.

"Hello," Monika said tentatively.

"Hello, Monika. This is Mike Black. Did I call at a bad time?"

"No. I don't get a lot of calls and I didn't recognize the number. In fact, I don't remember giving it to you. Not that it's a problem," Monika said quickly.

"Nick told it to me once."

"Once?"

"I'm good with numbers."

"Ooo–kay," she said like she didn't believe me, but I am. "So what's up?"

"Does the name Eileen McManus mean anything to you?"

"Eileen McManus? The name sounds familiar, but I don't know from where. Who is she?"

"I don't know. But see how she fits in with that thing we talked about."

"Got yah."

"Call me at this number if you get something."

"I will."

"And I haven't forgot about that other thing we talked about."

"See that you don't," Monika said and ended the call.

When we got to the club, I made my way toward the office. The club was packed. As I pushed my way through the crowd I wondered if CeCe was in there somewhere. If she was she'd be sitting somewhere near the office. I didn't see her, but that didn't mean she wasn't there. I walked up the steps and thought about why I went out of my way to avoid her.

I was perfectly willing to fuck just about every other woman who set it out for me. Why not her? I thought about what she said the last time we talked. *I'm diggin' you, Mike Black. I think I've made that plain.*

I walked into Bobby's office and decided that I had too much goin' on to worry about that now. A convenient excuse, but it is what it is.

"What's up, Mike?" Bobby said, leaning back in his chair.

"I got something we need to talk about," I said and sat down.

"I don't like the sound of this already, what's up?"

"Angelo Collette came to see me tonight."

Bobby sat up straight. "Came to see you where?"

"At Cuisine. Just showed up at the door."

Bobby stood up and went to the bar. "What he want?" he asked and poured us a drink.

"He wanted to talk about Stark."

"He wants you to get them together or something?" Bobby handed me the glass and went behind his desk.

"He wants more than that, Bob. His exact words were that he was hopin' for something a little more than just an introduction."

"Like what?" Bobby asked and sat down.

"That he was thinkin' that maybe I would take more of an active role. I could be kind of a stabilizing influence. You know, keep problems down."

"What you tell him?"

"I told him that I would set up a meeting, but I would have to think about that influence shit."

"How'd he take it?"

"He said that he would consider it a personal favor if I would do that for him."

"What you gonna do?"

"You know what I'm gonna do. I'm gonna tell him no."

"How do you think he'll take that?"

"I don't know."

"Angelo has done a lot for you over the years."

"I know. How do I say no?"

"First off, what does he mean by stabilizing influence?"

"I didn't ask him."

Bobby laughed. "Wasn't tryin' to hear that shit, were you?"

"No." I laughed too, but the shit wasn't funny. "This couldn't happen at a worse time."

"I know. Why now, when he knows we're tryin' to go another way? Why drop that shit on you now?"

"I wish I knew for sure, Bob. What I do know is that Angelo has problems of his own."

"With who?"

"FBI, DEA, I didn't ask him and I didn't wanna know. But he wants to do business with Stark."

"But he doesn't want that heat now."

"That's where we come in."

"You gotta think that what he means by stabilizing influence is that you deal with Stark. Any problems come up, you deal with it. Any heat, you catch it."

"Naturally, I could charge a fee for my services."

"Naturally."

"What do you think we should do?"

"You know," Bobby said and took a sip of his drink. "My first thought is that we should go ahead and do it."

"But—"

"But I'm only thinking about the money. With Angelo behind Stark, and with our muscle and organization, we should takeover the city. At that point it's just business. Same business we used to be a part of."

"But—" I said and Bobby cut me off again.

"But, with that comes the flipside. The cops and the fuckin' DEA start looking at you." Bobby paused. "You know when you first came to me and said you wanted to get out of the dope game, I wasn't for it."

"I remember."

"But I went along. Now I truly believe that it was the best decision we ever made. We're not in jail because nobody cares if a muthafucka loses his money gambling or borrows money or he gets some pussy. They think what we do is a harmless vice. And as long as we payoff the right people, nobody bothers us."

"I agree. It's what put us in a position to move this thing to the left."

"I was startin' to get into this legit thing; having meetings with Meka Brazil. That's a bad bitch. By the why, if you're not gonna fuck her I will," Bobby promised.

"Go ahead; it's a free country, Bob. Go for it, but I don't think she likes you."

"I don't think she does, either. But that's what makes it fun."

"Whatever, Bob. So you agree with me, you don't think we should do it?"

"I don't know. But here again, I'm only thinkin' about the money."

"Is the money worth what we stand to lose?"

"No. So, what you gonna do?"

"I'll setup the meeting with Stark and back away."

"Then what?"

"I'll think of something. Then there's Martin Marshall."

"What his punk-ass got to do with this?"

"Nothing. I went to see him about Vinnelli tonight."

"I thought you were lettin' that go?"

"I can't. Not until he's dead."

Bobby shook his head. "What about Martin?"

"He's running for Congress. Vinnelli can tie him to De-Francisco and Diego's mess. Vinnelli's a loose end that he can't afford."

"That's where you come in. You take care of Vinnelli for him. You were gonna kill him anyway."

"He said he was expecting me."

"What?"

"Said he knew after I took care of DeFrancisco that I'd come back to him to get Vinnelli."

"That makes sense."

"He knew that we're responsible for Mylo and Masters. He even knew that I had Monika tryin' to get something on Vinnelli."

Bobby's expression changed. "How's old sexy one-eye doin', anyway? I wouldn't mind fuckin' her ass either."

"Is there anybody you wouldn't mind fuckin'?"

"Yes, but she ain't one of them. But anyway, how's Martin know all that shit?"

"I'm glad you caught that. The answer is, I don't know. Martin's been a state senator for a long time. We have no idea how much power he's carryin' or how more powerful he'd be if he wins this election. That's the direction we need to be movin' in."

"So you got Angelo on one side and Martin on the other. Martin can't afford for you to be hooked up with Angelo or Stark."

"So I tell Angee no, and I kill Vinnelli for Martin."

"After you kill Vinnelli, Martin's gonna want you dead too."

"Assassinate the assassin."

"You tell Angelo no and he'll do it for him."

"Either way, I'm fucked." I picked up the phone and dialed Nick's cell phone. When he didn't answer I called Kevon.

"Hello."

"On my way, boss."

When Kevon got to the office I told him to keep callin' Nick until he got him and tell him to meet us there as soon as he could.

Chapter 29

Nick

I opened my eyes slowly and scanned the room. At first I
didn't know where I was. I took a look at the clock. It
was 10:45 in the morning. The second thing slapped me
in the face. I grabbed my head with one hand and cov-
ered my eyes with the other to block out the sun. I had a
serious head-throbbing hangover, and sunshine was the
last thing I needed after last night.

Rain was lying next to me with the covers pulled over
her head, gliding her hand up and down my hardening
erection. "Good morning," I said.

"Hey." Was all Rain had to offer, and continued what
she was doing. "What time is it?"

"Ten forty-five."

"Hmm."

"I know how you feel. My head is killin' me."

"Why you think I got this sheet over my head? Too
fuckin' bright in here. Thin-ass fuckin' curtains."

"How long you been up?"

"Not long. Long enough to get this dick hard. Why
don't you come under here and join me?"

I pulled the cover over my head and rolled over on my side. I looked at Rain. She was lying on her side with her eyes closed. Her look was softer and her body was beautiful.

Rain let go of my dick and rolled onto her back. Then she allowed her hands to move freely over her body. I looked on as Rain very deliberately spread her lips with her thumb and forefinger and made small circles around her clit. I moved down so I could get a closer look.

After awhile she stopped and reached out with both hands and grabbed my head. Rain raised her legs while slowly lowering my head between her thighs at the same time. I kissed her inner-thighs and tasted the wetness between them. I slid my tongue inside her and sucked her moist lips gently. I felt her body quiver and her clit grew harder, her thighs pressed together. "Yeah," Rain let out as her body convulsed.

Rain held my head in place while my tongue slithered along her lips, making circles around her clit. Her grip grew tighter. "Shit!" Rain mumbled and moaned her approval. I gripped her thighs with both hands, and positioned her body. My hands ran along the length of her body, admiring the feel of her skin.

Rain reached out from under the covers and returned with a condom. She put a condom on and then straddled me. With her eyes squeezed shut, she rode me slowly. I could feel myself getting harder, ready to bust as I felt her ass bucking, pounding against me. Her muscles locked and she drained me. "Yeah—that's right."

It was after one o'clock when we left the hotel. I got in the car and felt around for my phone. As expected I had missed calls. Wanda called once this morning and Kevon had called ten times. I glanced over at Rain and knew I wasn't calling Wanda back right then, so I called Kevon.

"What's up, Nick," Kevon answered.

"What's up? You called me?"

"Yes, sir. Black need to see you."

"Where is he?"

"He'll be at Cuisine in the next hour, maybe two. If you get there and he not there, him ask that you please wait for him."

"I'll be there," I said and ended the call.

"Where you gotta go now?"

"I gotta meet Black at Cuisine."

"Mike Black."

Why does every woman say his name like that?

"You know him?"

"Nope, but I seen him around. Pops thinks a lot of him. Says Black's one of the few people around these days got some honor left in what he does."

"All true."

"You gonna introduce me to him?"

"I hadn't planned on it. I was gonna drop you off and go meet him."

"Drop me off where? I don't wanna go back to my apartment yet."

"Wherever you want."

Rain folded her arms across her chest and sighed. "I know you got shit to do, but could you take me by a mall or some place I could get some clothes? I don't wanna get dropped off no place lookin' like this. I look like I been fuckin' all night."

I looked at Rain. Her hair was a mess and she had no makeup on. Since I ripped it open the night before, she had tied her blouse in the front, and her nipples were pressing against the material.

"I mean, you tore the buttons off this shirt, and I came out of my bra and panties before we left my apartment."

I looked at the clock on the dash. "I could do that." It was the least I could do under the circumstances.

We drove to Cross County Mall and since I hate shopping, I took a seat on a bench and told Rain to go on
without me. "But don't take too long."

"I know, you got someplace to be," Rain said and
walked off.

As soon as she was out of sight, I took out my phone
and called Wanda. Thankfully, she didn't ask me any questions that I had to lie about. She said that she missed me
and that Kevon was looking for me earlier.

"I talked to him. I gotta meet Black at Cuisine in about
an hour."

"I gotta go, but I was hoping that you could make
some time for me tonight."

"Sounds good. But let me see what Black wants before
I say yes or no."

"He wants to talk to you about Charles Watson. I
checked it out like you asked and Mike is interested."

"Then I'd say I'm probably gonna be busy tonight."

"I understand that, but you gotta sleep some time.
Come by when you're done. I need to see you. I mean, I
really need to see you. I gotta go now, Nick, but come
over tonight. It doesn't matter what time," Wanda said
and hung up the phone.

I put my phone back in my pocket and thought about
Wanda and what I had done with Rain the night before.
Right or wrong, I had no regret about having sex with
Rain. We both got what we wanted, and from the way we
went at it, it was what we both needed.

The question was what now? What was gonna happen
with me and Rain? I could drop her off wherever she
wanted to be dropped off and be done with it.

The thing was, I liked Rain, enjoyed being with her, enjoyed sittin' around talkin' shit with her. I had to laugh
though, 'cause every time we've been together we've

killed somebody. And maybe that was part of the attraction.

Since I was out here with time to kill, I went by Bath & Body Works. Mrs. Phillips told me that Zakiya used to work there, so I went in hoping to learn something that would help me find her killer.

After talking with her manager, I went and reclaimed my spot of the bench. Like everybody else, her manager had nothing but high praise for Zakiya. What a wonderful person she was; a hardworking, dependable employee. That was Zakiya. But she was only working there part-time. Whoever Nice N. Slow was, he had money. All useful information, but moved me no closer to my objective.

It was over an hour later when Rain came walking up.

"How do I look?"

She was wearing a black sleeveless dress and heels to match. Her hair was pulled back in a ponytail and her face was made up.

"You look very nice." She really did.

"You like this dress? It's an Anne Klein taffeta dress."

"I like it," I said and started for the car. "It looks good on you."

"Sorry it took me so long, but I had to do something with my hair and get some make up."

"I understand," I said as I got in the car, but I didn't. I have never understood why it takes women so long to shop. "Where you want me to drop you off?"

"In a hurry to get rid of me now, huh?"

"I'm not in a hurry to get rid of you," I promised, but I was ready for her to go.

"I know you got some place you gotta be, so you can take me back to the club."

"Cool," I said and drove off in that direction.

On the way there my phone rang. I looked at the display; it was Kevon calling.

"Hello."

"Black here over an hour waiting for you. How long 'fore you reach?"

"I'll be there in fifteen minutes." I hung up the phone and looked at Rain. "I need to get to this meeting—"

"I'm in no hurry. I got no place to be. Go on and handle your business. I hear the food is good there and I'm hungry. You can't fuck me all night and not feed me. What kinda bitch you think I am?" Rain said with a smile.

"The kind that ain't thought nothin' about food while she was up fuckin' all night."

"You're right. But right now, you ain't fuckin' me, so I'm hungry. So unless you plannin' on pullin' this XLR over and goin' up in me, you need to just go on to your meeting. You talk to Black and I'll eat."

I was kind of reluctant to take Rain with me on the off chance that Wanda might be there. I thought about telling Rain how to play it in case she was, but I decided to tackle that when it came up.

It was after four when we got to Cuisine. They weren't open yet, but I told Rain I'd see if there was somebody there that could fix something for her. "You have a seat at the bar and try not to shoot anybody."

"Very funny. You get them to feed me or it might be you I kill," Rain said as I walked away from her.

Black was seated at a table near the bar and I made my way to him. On the way, I stopped Lexi, the manager, and asked her to take care of Rain. When I got to the table, Kevon got up and walked away.

"I was gonna ask where you been, but I see," Black said when I sat down.

"Sorry. I left my phone in the car. What's up?"

Black told me about Angelo and his visit to Cuisine the night before. I was surprised. Not by Angelo's request. It was a smart move on his part. The right move at the right time. No, what surprised me was that Black was even considering it.

We kicked it back and forth for awhile, each of us running through hypothetical situations. At the end, we both agreed that each hypothetical always ended the same way: In jail or dead.

"I ain't goin' to jail, Nick. We already got enough problems with the DEA without this. Last thing we need right now is them crawling all over us again."

"So what are you gonna tell Angelo?"

"I been thinking about that. How I can give Angee what he wants without actually doin' shit."

I laughed. "How you plan on doin' that?"

"I'm gonna get him and Stark together and then I'm gonna tell him that I would offer advice and counsel to Stark as a personal favor to him. But for reasons that I know he understands, I can't go any further than that."

"You think that will satisfy him?"

"As long as I can get Stark to do business and as long as I can control him. But for that to work, you gotta be my guarantee. You gotta make sure that nothing we do touches that. We can't have our hands dirty in none of that."

"I'll stay on top of it."

"I haven't said anything about this to Wanda. But she was there when Angelo came to Cuisine, so she knows something's up. She wasn't happy with the answer I gave her, so she'll be coming at you. But she doesn't need to know anything about this."

"Understood."

"Everything else all right?" Black asked.

"Yeah, everything else is fine."

"I want you to go ahead and take care of that thing with Watson we discussed."

"Wanda mentioned that you did. It's already in motion."

"Who's your friend?"

"Rain Robinson."

"So that's Rain Robinson. She looks like her daddy," Black observed.

"Yeah, I noticed. I saw a picture of her mother and she definitely looks like her father."

"Barbara Robinson."

"You knew her?"

"No, just heard the stories."

"What stories?"

"One of the great thug mysteries of all time: Who killed Barbara Robinson? You never heard this story?"

"No."

"The story goes that Barbara used to fuck around with a low-rent pimp named Eddie Mars. Then J.R. comes along, falls hard for her, and sweeps her off her feet. They get married like a couple of months later. But the word was that Barbara was still in love with Eddie and was still fuckin' him—fucked him on her wedding day. But anyway, Barbara gets pregnant. Now when the baby is born J.R. goes crazy 'cause the kid doesn't look anything like him."

"Miles looks like his mother."

"Well, J.R. is convinced that the baby looks like Eddie, and he beats Barbara's ass at the hospital and goes after Eddie."

"Did he kill him?"

"No. They fired a few shots at each other and after that, Eddie just stayed out of J.R.'s way. Next thing you know, Barbara is pregnant again. So when your girl is born, J.R. is cool 'cause she looks just like him. Everything is cool for awhile, but J.R. starts hearin' that Barbara is seeing Eddie behind his back again. Couple of days later, cops find Barbara and Eddie dead at a motel. Murder-suicide. She shot him twice: once in the dick and once in the chest. Then she shot herself. But the word was that J.R. followed them to that motel and killed them both."

"It's just like the man said; two-faced woman and a jealous man."

"Cause of the trouble since the world began," Black said finishing the line from the James Brown song then stood up. "I gotta get outta here." He looked in Rain's direction and sat back down. "Look, Nick, I know this is none of my business, and far be it for me to tell you who to lay the pipe to. Especially when I'm fuckin' every woman with a fat-ass and big titties I run into. Just don't hurt Wanda." Black stood up again.

"I won't."

I introduced Black to Rain and walked with him as he left Cuisine. Since I was hungry, I went back inside and joined Rain for a meal. I would drop her off after I was full.

Chapter 30

I went in the kitchen and had the cook make me a Porter-house steak, medium, smothered in onions and mush-rooms. While I ate, I talked to Rain, but mostly I thought about what I was gonna do to Charles Watson and how I would do it. When I finished eating, I thought about Freeze. I could use him for what I had planned.

"You're kind of quiet," Rain said. "What you thinkin' about?"

"I gotta do something tonight. Something me and Freeze woulda handled."

"You miss your road dog. I know how that feels."

I looked at Rain. "Yeah, I guess you do. Your road dog's in jail." Maybe that was part of the attraction. We needed each other.

"Right."

We left Cuisine and I headed in the direction of J.R.'s.

"Tell me about your dog. What he go down for?"

"His name is Jarreau, but everybody calls him Jay Easy. He got cracked over some stupid shit. Me and him just got through takin' care of a problem, you understand.

When we split up, I gave him the guns 'cause they was both hot, and told him to get rid of them. But before he got to do it, he decides he needs to stop and get some cigarettes. When he leaves the store, he gets pulled over. Cops search the car, find the guns. Guns got bodies on them. Jay Easy goes down for murder."

"Over a pack of cigarettes?"

"Over a pack of cigarettes. You know that nigga quit smokin' after that." Rain laughed. "But the nigga stood tall; never said a word about me being with him."

"That's how you got around to using me."

"Shit, I think we make a good team."

I hated to admit it, but she was right, so I told her. "Yeah, we do."

"In more ways than one," Rain said and pushed her lips out at me.

"I been there for you; I been your road dog. Time for you to return the favor."

"What you want me to do?" Rain asked eagerly.

I explained to Rain what was going on and how I wanted the night to go. She moaned when I told her what I wanted her to do.

On the way there we stopped on Fordham Road. I told Rain that we needed to buy a black scarf, some big dark sunglasses, some leather gloves, and a big purse. "Why?"

" 'Cause I don't need them knowing who you are. None of this needs to link you to me. A black scarf 'cause it will go with that sexy dress. We need the purse to carry the hardware."

Rain smiled. "You wearing a mask?"

"No, I want them to know who I am."

We arrived at the Watson house and waited for the lady of the house to get there. It was a big five-bedroom house in a nice neighborhood.

I parked the car down the street, but close enough to see the house. "Come on. Bring the purse," I said and got out.

I went around to the trunk and opened it. Then I took the panel out of the back. I handed a gun to Rain. "Bersa Thunder .380 compact pistol, semi-automatic; single or double action, 3.5 inch barrel, seven-round capacity. Start with that."

"Sweet," Rain said and put one in the chamber. I put the rest of what we'd need in the purse and closed the panel. I handed the purse to Rain. "That's not too heavy is it?"

"No," Rain said and flexed her muscle.

We got back in the car and watched the house. While we waited, Rain found creative ways to pass the time. I looked at the clock.

"She should be here soon."

"What's she drivin'?"

"Silver C class Benz. Two-thirty I believe."

"Coming down the street right now."

We watched Watson's wife go inside the house.

"Give her some time to get settled," I told Rain and she began tying the scarf around her head. When nothing but her round face was showing, Rain put on the sunglasses.

"How do I look?"

"Famous. Can you see?"

"See enough to do what I gotta do. You ready?"

"I'm right behind you."

We put on our gloves, Rain got out of the car and we made the short walk to the house. While I stood off to the side, Rain rang the bell. When the door opened, Rain smiled. "Mrs. Watson?"

"Yes."

Rain shoved the .380 under her chin. "Step inside. And

do it quietly. If you scream I will kill you right now and not give a fuck." She backed Mrs. Watson in the house. I looked around and closed the door behind us.

When I got in the house, Rain had Mrs. Watson backed up against the wall and had the gun to her head. "I don't have much money here," she said.

"Do I look like I came here for money? You say anymore dumb shit like that I swear I'll put a bullet in your eye. Understand?"

"Yes," Mrs. Watson said quietly.

"Understand!" Rain yelled.

"Yes!" Mrs. Watson yelled back and she began to cry.

"Now go in the living room and sit down."

Rain walked Mrs. Watson into the living room and I followed quietly behind them. She shoved her into a chair, while I took a seat on the couch. Rain put the purse on the coffee table in front of me. I made sure Mrs. Watson was looking at me before I opened the bag slowly. I took out a Kel-Tec PLR-16 semi-automatic pistol: single action, .223 Remington caliber shells, 9.2-inch barrel, with ten-round capacity. I put the magazine in and set it down on the coffee table in front of me.

Then I took out a Smith & Wesson 1911 .45 pistol, with a black and silver finish and handed it to Rain.

"Thank you," she said and returned her attention to Mrs. Watson. "Do you wanna die tonight?" Rain asked and pointed the gun at her head.

"No."

"It's a good day to die, so if you do, tell me now."

"No, no. I don't want to die," she said shaking head and the tears began to flow again.

"Good. The only way to keep me from killin' you is to do exactly what I say. Understand me?"

"Yes."

"You be a good girl and do what I say and you might

live through the night. But I gotta tell you, there's more to it then just you." Rain picked up the phone. "See, you're gonna call your husband and tell him anything, but get him to come home right away. When he gets here, I need him to be a good boy, so it's up to you to make sure he does. Of course that ain't always the easiest thing in the world 'cause you know how boys get? They gotta man up, you know. Act all tough and shit. Beatin' their chest, you know what I'm sayin'. Let their balls hang," Rain said and laughed. Mrs. Watson cracked a smile too.

"But that's the wrong thing for him to do. 'Cause you see, that shit will get both of y'all killed. The last thing you see will be your husband gettin' two to the head before I shoot you. So you need to convince him that he needs to pay attention. Listen very carefully to what is being told to him and make the right decision. Okay?"

"Okay," Mrs. Watson said and shook her head.

"But making the right decision is important 'cause make the wrong decision and I'll kill y'all." Rain looked at me. "I don't give a fuck. I'm just the hired help."

Rain stepped closer and put the barrel of her gun between Mrs. Watson's eyes.

"You think you can do that?"

Mrs. Watson shook her head with her eyes closed tightly.

"Good. But first I need you to call Clay Barksdale and tell him that your husband wants to see him at the house, right away."

"What should I tell them it's about?"

"I don't give a fuck what you tell them," Rain said and pressed the gun to her forehead again. "Just get them over here now!" Rain screamed and handed her the phone.

Mrs. Watson did as she was told and called Barksdale. She was surprisingly calm about it for somebody that had a gun to her head. When he said he was on his way, I took a few pairs of plastic handcuffs out of the purse and handed them to Rain.

I stood up with the Tec-16 in my hands and pointed it at Mrs. Watson while Rain put the cuffs around her wrists. Rain left the room and when she came back she had a chair from the dining room. She positioned it in front of the couch, and then told Mrs. Watson to go make herself comfortable.

While we waited for Barksdale to show up, Rain took the chair Mrs. Watson was in and talked shit to her. I stood by the window and watched out for him. I looked at Rain. She got up and was wandering around the living room—talking shit. I liked the way she worked. I would definitely use her again.

Rain stopped in front of a picture of two teenagers.

"These your kids?" she asked.

Mrs. Watson nodded her head quickly. "They're away at college," she informed us.

"Good looking kids." Rain brought me the picture. I glanced at the boy and girl and handed it back to Rain.

When I saw Barksdale's car pull up in front of the house, I signed for Rain to cut Mrs. Watson's cuffs and walk her to the door.

She opened the door slowly and Barksdale came in. "Hey Frankie, how you doing? I see Charlie ain't here yet." It was at that second that he felt the barrel of Rain's gun at the back of his neck.

"You just keep walking," she instructed. I stepped out so he could see me with the Tec-16 in one hand and a .9 miller in the other, just in case he thought about trying Rain. "Sit down in that chair and don't make a fuckin' sound," she demanded.

Barksdale complied with Rain's request and sat in the

chair in front of the couch. I kept my guns on him while Rain put duct tape over his mouth, and cuffed his arms behind his back and his ankles to the chair.

Rain handed the phone to Mrs. Watson. "Call your husband." She, too, complied with Rain's request. Rain cuffed Mrs. Watson's hands in front of her and sent her back to the couch to wait. Then we made ourselves comfortable.

It didn't take long before Watson walked through the front door. "Frankie, Frankie."

Rain was in place and put a gun to his head. "Not Frankie. Why don't you go inside and sit down next to your wife." She walked Watson into the living room.

"What's going on here?" Watson said and Rain hit him so hard in the back of his head that he dropped to one knee.

Rain pressed the barrel against his forehead and got in his face. "You don't say a muthafuckin' thing, unless I muthafuckin' tell you to! You got that?"

Watson nodded his head.

"Now get up and go sit down like I told you to."

Watson got up and Rain pushed him in the direction of the couch. "You better tell this muthafucka what time it is, Frankie. This muthafucka wanna get y'all niggas killed."

"Just do what they tell you, Charlie, please."

"What's goin' on, Frankie?" Watson said quietly.

"Just sit down and be quiet, Charlie, please," she pleaded with him. Watson did as his wife said and sat down next to her.

After Rain put plastic cuffs on Watson's wrists and ankles and duct tape over both their mouths, it was time for the show to begin. I stood up and ripped open Barksdale's shirt. For the next hour or so, the Watson's watched in horror as I beat Barksdale and burned his chest with acid.

When Barksdale finally passed out, I went and got another chair from the dining room and placed it close to the Watson's. Once I sat down, I looked at Rain.

"Wake him up."

Rain reached back and backhanded Barksdale. His head snapped back and his eyes jerked open.

"Now kill him."

Rain put the gun to his head. You could see the fear in his eyes and terror in the Watson's. She fired once. The impact knocked the chair over.

I told Rain to take the duct tape off Watson's mouth.

"Do you know who I am?"

"No."

"My name is Nick Simmons. Howard Owens works for me."

"I was gonna pay him his money. I just need a little more time."

I looked at Rain. She stepped up quickly and punched Watson in the mouth. "What I say about talkin', huh? You don't say a muthafuckin' thing, unless I muthafuckin' tell you to!" she said and hit him again.

"You had your chance to pay Howard. You had your chance to pay the two gentlemen I sent to talk to you last week, but you ducked out on them and then you sent that asshole to rough-up Howard's brother and take a shot at him. That's why he's layin' there dead now. When you shoot, shoot to kill not scare!" I said to the dead man.

"You don't owe that money to Howard anymore. Now you owe me. So here's what's gonna happen. I own ten percent of your business. Tomorrow morning I'm gonna send the same two men around to your office at ten o'clock and you're gonna be there to meet them. You're gonna give them the money you owe, including the interest, and they're gonna give you some papers to sign.

Sign them. The next morning another man will be there. He is my representative, he'll explain how things are gonna work. The good news is you still run the company, but you don't do shit unless you talk to him first. Do we have a deal or do I have to kill your wife?"

Watson didn't answer at first; he just looked at Rain. Mrs. Watson nudged her husband. Rain laughed a little and nodded her head. "We have a deal," Watson said and dropped his head.

"Smart man. Do what I say and you'll live a lot longer and you'll make a lot more money," I said and got up. "By the way, if you even think about callin' the cops and sayin' anything about our deal, I promise you that you will get to watch me kill your wife and those two kids, before I cut your head off. Do we have an understanding?"

Watson looked at Rain again for permission to speak. When she nodded her head, Watson said, "Yes, I understand."

We left the Watson's tied up with a dead body in the middle of their living room floor. Once we got back to the car and drove away, Rain turned to me.

"Let's get a room and fuck."

Chapter 31

I rolled out of bed and quickly got in the shower. When I was finished I got dressed. While I put my clothes on, I looked at Rain lying naked on the bed.

"I gotta go," I said and ran my hand along her hip and down her thigh.

"You got a woman, don't you?" Rain asked without looking up.

"Yes."

"Go handle your business." Rain rolled over on her back, spread her legs, and made it just that much harder for me to leave. "I'll see you tomorrow?"

"You will," I said and rushed out of there.

It was after two in the morning when I unlocked the door to Wanda's house. On the way there, I ran through several scenarios in my mind. Trying to prepare my answers to whatever questions Wanda was going to throw at me.

The reason men get caught cheating is that they don't have their story straight and can't remember what story they told when they did, so the story always changes.

Men think of their excuse on the way home, like I had done.

It's different with a woman. Before a woman leaves the house, she has her story down-pat, her alibi in place, and her answers ready for the few questions we men do ask. And her story never changes. No matter how many holes it may have, that's her story and she'll stick to it, sometimes even when there is evidence to the contrary.

Wanda was asleep when I slipped into the bedroom. I looked at her lying there on her side in a black silk gown, and then thought about Rain lying naked in almost the same position. I got undressed quietly and even though I had just taken one, I got in the shower. I always took a shower before I got in bed with Wanda, and that night wasn't the night I was going to break that tradition.

I stood in the shower and lathered up from head to toe to get the smell and feel of motel soap off of me. As the water rolled off my body, I gave some thought to the fact that this was the first time I had been with another woman since Wanda and I had been together.

Part of that was Wanda, being insanely jealous, went out of her way to keep women away from me. But the other part was that I was, and I guess still am, happy with the relationship and the sex we have. So if that's the case, why did I spend the last two nights fuckin' Rain? And why was I thinkin' about fuckin' her fine young-ass again tomorrow?

I didn't have an answer, so I got out of the shower.

When I slid in between the sheets, Wanda began to stir. "Hi, babe," Wanda said quietly and rolled closer to me.

"Hi. Sorry I woke you."

"That's all right. I would have been mad if you didn't," Wanda said and started kissing me.

While we made love, thoughts and images of Rain popped in my mind, as they did with Wanda while I was inside Rain. But instead of forcing them out of my mind, I focused on them.

Rain likes to masturbate in front of me, and I gotta admit it sets me the fuck off. If Wanda did masturbate, and I'm sure she does, I've never seen it, and doubt seriously if I ever will. And I'm cool with that. There is so much more to Wanda than just her sex.

But I could make the same argument about Rain. Granted, it would be a different argument because they are two completely different women. Wanda was a corporate lawyer with gangster impulses. Rain was all gangster; all the time. And there was definitely more to her than just her fat ass and those juicy nipples. The way she handled the Watson's was impressive. Rain was impressive.

Handle your business. I'll see you tomorrow.

When I woke up and looked at the clock it was almost noon. I looked around the room and was surprised to see Wanda sitting in the chair across from the bed.

Now it comes.

"Good morning," she said as soon as I made eye contact with her.

"Morning, Wanda," I yawned and closed my eyes.

"Did you sleep well?"

"Very." I wanted to ask her what she was still doing there, or why hadn't she gone to the office, but there was no rush. Wanda would get to her purpose for being there soon enough.

"How did it go with Watson?"

"By now Jap and Kenny should be at your office with the papers."

"That's good. Controlling that company will put us in a better position to bid on steel contracts."

"I'm happy when my work makes your job easier."

"It will also make us more money, so your work pays you back in the long run."

"Good to know," I said and rolled over.

"How'd your meeting go with Mike?"

"Fine."

"Did he talk to you about what Angelo wanted?"

"Did Angelo want something?"

Wanda hesitated. "He came by the club the other night."

"Which club?"

"Cuisine. Mike said he's been inviting Angelo to Cuisine since it opened and then he just showed up there."

"Maybe he was just in the neighborhood."

"Or it could be something important."

"I'm sure if it was important he would have mentioned it to you."

"I don't think so. Lately he's been saying that it doesn't look right for me to be in my position and be advising a criminal organization."

"He's right."

"I know."

"I mean you're the one draggin' him kickin' and screamin' to that side of the house."

"He hasn't even been kickin' and screamin'."

"Black likes to make money, bottom line. You showed him the money and he's moving that way. Isn't that what you wanted?"

"Yes. But I still feel so left out."

"You'll be all right."

"That's what he says."

"He's right, you will."

"So who was that woman with you?"

Now it comes.

My first instinct was to say, what woman? But I know who she's talkin' about and she knows I know who she's talkin' about. Me asking what woman would only piss her off and send this conversation down the road to perceived denial and deception. No, take it head on. "That was Rain Robinson."

"Who is she, Nick?"

"She's J.R. Robinson's daughter."

"What were you doing having dinner with her?"

"She's helping me find who killed Zakiya Phillips."

"Who?"

"The woman who was killed at Paradise Fish and Chicken. You remember I told you that Black wanted me to look into it."

"Yeah, but I'm sure he wasn't expecting you to waste a lot of time on it."

"Black told me that he didn't want people thinkin' that now that Freeze is dead that they could just hit our spots and we don't do nothing about it."

"I understand that, but we've got plenty of people that could handle that mess."

"That's true. But he wants me to establish myself, handle things personally."

"What does you handling things personally have to do with you having dinner with her?"

"Nothing. How many men do you have lunch and dinner with?"

"That's business."

"So is this."

"How?"

"I told you, she's helping me find the guys that murdered Zakiya Phillips."

"What is she, a private detective?" Wanda asked sarcastically. "How is she helping you?"

"My sources say that some of J.R.'s people were involved in it."

"And?"

"I went to see J.R. Talked to him about it and he assured me that he didn't know anything about it. But

since he doesn't want any bad blood with Black, he told
Rain to help me find who did it."

Wanda folded her arms across her chest and that pouty
look came over her face; which meant that at least for the
time being, I had successfully held her off. "I still don't
like you having dinner with her."

"What's wrong with it? We were hungry, so we ate. And
if you want to get technical about it, we didn't have dinner together. She ate while I talked to Black and then she
sat and watched me eat. But you already know that," I
said and made a mental note to keep Rain out of all of
our spots. Wanda had eyes everywhere, and I need to
know who they are.

I had to ask myself as Wanda got up and got ready to
leave, if that meant I planned on Rain being around for
awhile?

The answer was yes.

"When am I gonna see you again?" Wanda asked.

"I'll see you tonight," I promised as my cell phone
rang.

Wanda looked at me.

I looked at her.

The phone rang again.

"Aren't you gonna answer it?"

I got out of bed and got the phone from my pants
pocket. I looked at the display, but didn't recognize the
number.

I looked at Wanda again and her eyes narrowed.

"Hello."

"You busy?" Rain asked.

"Yes."

"Tell your woman I said hello," Rain suggested.

"No."

"Yeah, well, I know where we can find the two niggas
you looking for. But I don't know how long they gonna

be in play, so if you want them we need to get them
now."

"Where are you?"

"I'm at the hotel where you left me, nigga. Come get
me and let's go get these niggas."

"I'm on my way," I said and ended the call.

"Who was that?"

"That was Rain."

"What does she want?"

"She's got a line on the guys I'm lookin' for," I said and
headed for the shower. The next sound I heard was
Wanda slamming the door.

The first round went to me. But I knew as long as I
kept seeing Rain that Wanda would be back at me and
this fight would continue.

When I picked up Rain, she told me that the bandits
were holed up in some apartments in the south Bronx.
"How'd you find out where to find them?"

" 'Cause niggas talk."

"What you mean?"

"I mean last night they were talkin' about it."

"To who?"

"Damn, why I gotta give up all that?"

"To who?"

"Like I said, last night at a strip club in Manhattan that
a friend of mine dances at; she said this guy was braggin'
to her that he was a robber, and this and that, and that
he's robbed everything from banks to fish and chicken
joints for small change. He does it for the rush, not the
money. But she says he was flashin' plenty of money. So
she asks him if he ever killed anybody. He said if the
money is right. Then he said, sometimes the robbin' is
just to cover the hit."

"That's all you got?"

"It's more than you got."

"They your people?"

"No, but I know some people that know them."

"I hate to even have to ask you this, but this ain't more of your personal shit, is it?"

"I hate you gotta ask me that shit too. I thought we were past that; especially after last night. If I needed you to go down with me on some shit, I would tell you. So no," Rain said with an attitude. "This is not more of my personal shit."

"Sorry."

"Accepted."

When we got to the building we went inside. On the way up the steps Rain asked, "How you wanna do this?"

"I don't know, but I want them alive. If these are the guys, and the robbery was just to cover the hit, I want to know who hired them."

"Then *we'll* kill them." Rain smiled.

When we got to their floor we could hear somebody blastin' their music. As we got closer to the apartment it was obvious that the music was coming from there.

Rain and I stood off to the side of the door with our guns out and I banged on it a few times, but nobody answered. "Kick it in," Rain suggested.

I tried the doorknob instead.

The door was unlocked.

"That works too," she commented as I opened the door and went in carefully. The fact that the door was opened and the music was playing didn't give me a good feeling. "Stay close to me," I whispered to Rain as we moved through the apartment.

When we got to the bedroom I opened the door slowly, halfway expecting to catch somebody fuckin'.

"Damn," I said and walked in the room.

Rain came in behind me. "Shit."

There before us in the bed lay two naked men; one with long dreads. They weren't fuckin', they were dead.

"From looks of it, somebody got them with an automatic weapon."

"So was the music to cover them fuckin' or to cover the sound of shooting?" Rain asked.

"I don't know, probably both." I walked over to the bed and tried to get a feel for how long they had been dead. "This happened sometime this morning."

"How do you know?"

"Rigor mortis has begun to set in. It begins about three hours after death, and lasts about seventy-two hours."

"That nice, but how do you know this?"

"Rigor mortis is caused by a chemical change in the muscles after death, causing the limbs of the corpse to become stiff. Come here, feel this."

"Oh, hell no. Let's get outta here," Rain said and left the room.

I followed her out of the bedroom and closed the door behind me, but we weren't leaving yet. "Search the place."

"What are we looking for?"

"Anything."

"Anything?"

We turned down the music and quickly searched the apartment looking for anything that confirmed that these were actually the men who shot Zakiya, or who paid them to do it. We didn't find anything.

Once again, I was back to square one and wondering how much more time I was gonna put into this. All I really had was a picture that she took at J.R.'s and some e-mail that could have been sent by anybody who worked at the club. I still felt that Nice N. Slow could be Miles. What I needed was to get a picture of him so I could show it to people at Paradise.

"Where you goin'?" Rain asked.

"I'm takin' you to the club."

"Good. I need to pick up my car; tired of you leavin' me stranded and shit." Rain ran her hand across my thigh and down to my crotch. "Unless you wanna go get a room first."

It was after five when we left the room. I drove Rain to the club and hoped Miles would still be there. I got lucky. When we pulled up in the parking lot, Miles was just coming out of the building.

Rain got out of the car quickly and stopped Miles before he got to his car. I got out of the car, got a small camera out of the trunk and snapped a few shots of Miles. I spent the next couple of hours with Rain before I told her that I had to go.

Chapter 32

Mike Black

"Monika on the phone for you, boss," Kevon said and handed me the phone.

"What's up, Monika?

"I got something for you. Any way you can drop by here to see it?"

"I'm on my way," I told Monika and Kevon drove in that direction.

When we got to her apartment, Kevon turned off the car and turned to me. "You want me to come with you, boss?"

I thought for a minute. "Yeah, I think you should."

We went inside the building and up to her apartment. When Monika opened the door she looked surprised to see Kevon standing there with me. "Come on in," Monika said and walked away from the door. When Kevon closed the door, Monika turned around. "Your friend isn't coming in with you?"

"He waits at the door for me. Makes sure no one comes in on me."

Monika laughed. "Believe me, I got so much firepower in here that you'll be safe."

"So I heard. One day we'll have to have a conversation about you and your skills."

"Be sure that you do. I'd be very interested to hear what you have in mind for my skills," Monika said in a way that told me that I could fuck her right now. But I was there for business.

"What you got for me?"

"You were right. Eileen McManus is the key to everything."

"Who is she?"

"She's Vinnelli's mistress. I thought the name sounded familiar but couldn't place it. Her name is Amanda White. McManus is her maiden name, Eileen is her middle name."

"Mistress, huh?"

"Bad boy."

"Does his wife know?"

"Near as I can tell she doesn't."

"So what do you have on Eileen McManus?"

"Just about everything is in her name. He uses her to hide his money. I got financials on the offshore accounts he has."

"Is there any way to link it to him?"

"Yes. There's one company that filed for bankruptcy that lists Eileen McManus as CEO, and Vinnelli and De-Francisco as being on the board of directors. It was originally the holding company, for lack of a better term, that hid all their other shit. After DeFrancisco went to jail, Vinnelli got careful and cleaned up a lot. She sold off all the other companies and they changed hands through a series of dummy companies that move the money out of the country, and it all ends up back in her hands."

"How much money we talkin' about?"

"I'd say about seven or eight million, maybe more. Give me some time, I'm still looking."

"All of it in offshore accounts?"

"Pretty much."

"I guess this would be a good time to have that conversation about some of your skills."

"Okay, lets."

"How good are you?"

"I'm very good, Mr. Black. How good depends on what skill you're talkin' about."

"I want that money. Do you have the skills to get it?"

"As much as I'd like to say yes, I can't. Our old partner Jett Bronson could pull that off in his sleep."

"What about Travis Burns?"

"Yeah, maybe. I know he did that other thing for you with Diego, but this would be different."

"Not knowing a lot about computers, tell me why it would be different. And do it so I can understand it, please."

"See, that time Travis had a number of advantages. Knowing that a transaction was about to take place. He had access to the hardware the original transaction was run on, and he was able to get the password. That made it easy. So all he had to do was to go in behind them and transfer the money out. In this case, the money is, like I said, for the most part all offshore; mostly in the Caymans Islands, so he wouldn't have the same access or password. But that's just me thinking. Travis may be a badder boy than I give him credit for."

"See what you can do to make that happen."

"Yes, sir," Monika said and saluted me with a smile on her face.

I was about to leave when something she said crossed my mind. "One more thing."

"What's that?"

"That bankrupted holding company you told me about, Diego Estaban or Martin Marshall wouldn't be on that list of directors, would they?" I asked, thinking that as his position and power grows that I might need some leverage against Martin.

"No."

"I want you to look for anything that links Martin Marshall to Vinnelli or DeFrancisco."

"I'll do that. But I think I may already have that."

"What's that?"

"I found a draft of a leaked memo written by a Justice Department attorney named Ken Thomas. In the memo, Thomas alleges that DEA agents in Peru are in league with traffickers and are implicated in money laundering and murder. Thomas's allegations centered on an undercover operation called Peru-Man, which targeted traffickers in Peru and was overseen by DeFrancisco. At the time he was a DEA group supervisor in Miami. As part of that operation, DeFrancisco and the agents working under him, one of which was Vinnelli, had uncovered evidence that DEA agents in Peru appeared to be assisting traffickers in Peru."

"How does that relate to Marshall and how does it work for us?"

"I'm getting to that. But later that same year there were charges raised that led to DeFrancisco's operation being shut down."

"What was that?"

"There was an operation called White-Light that was setup to specifically target Diego Estaban and a Peruvian National Police colonel named Gonzalez."

"Diego, my old friend," I laughed.

"Estaban and Gonzalez were widely recognized to be involved in trafficking and arms dealing at the highest levels. Working with various sectors of the Peruvian military, they have fielded death squads responsible for murdering thousands of Peruvians."

"Now were gettin' somewhere."

"See, I told you. It all comes down to a meeting in Panama between Gonzalez and Vinnelli that was not coordinated properly with the Peru office. Vinnelli was instructed to contact the Peru office before finalizing a meeting with Gonzalez. Vinnelli had met with Gonzalez for two days in Panama without notifying the Peru office. DeFrancisco and Vinnelli offered different accounts of the meeting in Panama with Gonzalez."

"How so?"

"Vinnelli claims the meeting was unplanned. DeFrancisco told investigators that the meeting was not planned in advance. DeFrancisco said he recalled Vinnelli calling from Panama to report his interview of a big player; however, DeFrancisco could not remember if Vinnelli identified the player as Gonzalez. That put in motion a major criminal investigation targeting DeFrancisco and Vinnelli. DeFrancisco and Estaban were involved in a scheme with an informant named Isabelle Vega. She was going to testify about Diego's operation and that DeFrancisco and Vinnelli were extorting money from traffickers in exchange for promises of lenient jail sentences. But the report disappeared and Vega turned up dead. Vinnelli got a reprimand for the meeting and that squashed it."

"What does that have to do with Marshall?"

"It doesn't necessarily link Marshall to them, but it does link the two of them to Diego."

"Marshall and Diego were partners. So you would have to connect Marshall to Diego to link it to DeFrancisco and Vinnelli."

"Exactly. Then you add this conversation between Marshall and Diego." Monika made a few clicks on her laptop that I couldn't follow if I had to. "Listen to this."

The first voice I heard was Martin Marshall's. *"I don't want there to be any way this can come back and bite me."*

"You worry too much, my friend." That was Diego Estaban. *"Once the word begins to spread about his involvement in this business, his political allies will run for cover and you will have no need to fear him."*

"But if you can't find that package or it becomes public, it will put me and a lot of our friends in an extremely compromised position."

"If that happens, which it won't, because I assure you that the package will be recovered, we have set these things in motion so the spotlight will be on Mike Black and—" Diego laughed. I hated the way he laughed. I'm glad I killed him. *"—others, who I will make known to you when the time is right."*

"There is one other thing that concerns me."

"What is that, my friend?"

"DeFrancisco. He's shaky. I am not sure we can trust him to keep his mouth shut if anything goes wrong."

"How much does he really know? What have you told him?"

"I only told him what he needed to know to put the operation in motion. Still, he has me, and I don't need any more heat." That's Martin, always looking out for himself. *"I just got somebody else's stink off me."*

"He is your man. When he has outlived his usefulness you will have to insure his silence." I took care of that for him.

When the recording was over I smiled at Monika. "Where did you get that?"

"Travis recorded it while we were running surveillance on Marshall."

"I knew I liked that kid."

"He does impress sometimes."

"That's exactly what I need," I said to Monika and somebody knocked on her door.

"Excuse me a minute," she said and went to answer the door.

When she came back Monika said that it was Kevon knocking. "He said that Bobby called and needs to talk to you. He said it was important."

I stood up. "Let me go see what Bobby wants. You stay on this and talk to Travis about doing that other thing. We'll talk more about that after you talk to him."

Monika walked me to the door. "I'll call you if I get anything else I think you can use. Do you want me to take a look at Marshall?"

I thought about Marshall knowing that she was looking at Vinnelli. "Yes—and no." I took a step closer to Monika and leaned in close to her ear. "It was Marshall that gave me that name. When I talked to him, he told me that he knew you were looking at Vinnelli; said you were very talented."

"I'm flattered by the compliment, but that is not good. I'll try to cover my tracks a little better," Monika assured me. Then she thought for a second. Monika put her hands on my chest and I stepped closer as she whispered. "There might be another explanation. Other than me being sloppy, I mean. Felix and General Peterson used to work for Diego."

"Felix is the guy you and Nick used to work for, right?"

Nick told me about him. They used to call him Uncle Felix. I don't know why. After the rest of their unit was killed, they were flown back to Fort Brag, debriefed, and processed out. Uncle Felix approached them the next day. He told them that General Peterson, their former commanding officer, had recommended that he talk to them. He recruited them to do jobs for him that required their skills. It was Felix that set them up in a front business as private investigators.

"Right. Marshall was partners with Diego, so he had to know what we were doing in South America."

"And that you, Nick, and Jett survived," I whispered in her ear.

"He would know what skills we had, and he knows Nick works for you now."

"Which means he knows who you are—"

"And probably has somebody shadowing my on-line movements. It won't happen again."

"For the time bein', you stay on Vinnelli."

"Does that mean I can't, say, ask an old friend, say, in Israel, to stick his nose in?"

"No, it doesn't it mean that at all. I like the way you think. We'll talk soon," I said and left.

When I got in the car Kevon handed me the phone; it was already ringing. "Where you at?" Bobby asked as soon as he answered.

"Just leaving Monika's apartment."

"Did you fuck sexy one-eye?"

"No, I got her workin' on that thing for me."

"That don't mean you ain't fuckin' her."

"What you want, Bobby?"

"Did I miss a meeting today?"

"No."

"I just wanted to be sure."

"That's what was so important?"

"Yeah, that was it. You coming by the club tonight?"

"I don't know, maybe."

"CeCe was up here askin' for you the other night after you left."

"I'm not surprised." What surprised me was that she hadn't called since I gave her the number. "I'll get with you later," I said and ended the call.

I handed the phone back to Kevon. "Where to now, boss?"

"Let's go eat. I'm hungry."

Chapter 33

"Where you wanna go?" Kevon asked, sounding less than enthusiastic. The last couple of weeks I've been on this no-meat thing. Maria showed me a DVD about how eating a vegetable-based diet is much healthier than meat-based diets, because eating a meat-based diet puts you at higher risk for heart disease, some types of cancer, high-blood pressure, and shit like that. I don't know if I agree with the science behind it, but I do feel better since I stopped eating meat.

Since then, me and Maria have been dragging Kevon all over the city to these vegetarian restaurants. He hates it because Kevon is a hardcore carnivore. But tonight I felt like eating some meat.

"Let's go to the Blue Water Grill."

Kevon smiled because we'd eaten there before and he knew they served meat. "Refresh me memory."

"It's on Union and 16th Street. Call and make reservations."

On the way downtown I thought about what I had on Vinnelli and what I would do with it. Naturally, I wanted to take his money, but I wanted to hurt him, hurt him like he hurt me. I really wanted him dead. I just didn't want the problems that might come with that. So what was I gonna do?

Reservations and a couple of hundred dollars got us a table right away. The Blue Water Grill is a converted bank on Union Square. It used to be a restaurant called Metropolis and is one of the most popular restaurants in New York, according to the Zagat survey.

It was decorated with marble and dimly-lit red chandeliers that illuminate the dining room. There's an outdoor café and a subterranean lounge that features live jazz music.

As soon as our waitress got to the table Kevon said, "Filet Mignon." And put down the menu.

"And for you, sir, or are you going to need some time?" she turned to me and asked.

"You can bring me a Remy Martin VSOP and bring him one too. When you get back with those, I should be ready to order."

When the waitress returned with our drinks, I ordered the Blue Water Grill chopped salad and a couple of Maki Rolls. Spicy yellowtail and shrimp roll and spicy lobster, and tuna roll with avocado and jalapeños. I love jalapeños.

For my entrée I chose the grilled wild-striped bass, marinated with extra virgin olive oil, lemon, garlic and capers. Broccoli rabe and marinated farmers market vegetables. I was gonna get the lobster mashed potatoes, but I settled for the cream spinach.

We were just about done with our meal when Kevon pointed something out to me. "That woman there in the orange suit; she has been watching you for some time now."

"How do you know she's not watching you?"

"That was me first thought as well. So I watch her looking at you, until she see me watching her, then she look away."

I turned to see who he was talking about. She was very pretty, kind of classy. The longer I looked the more she looked like I knew her from somewhere. She was sitting with an older white man, having drinks, and talking. When we made eye contact she smiled and raised her glass. I picked up mine and did the same.

"I told you. The woman has been watching you all evening," Kevon said.

"Like I know her from somewhere."

"Want me to ask her where you know her from, boss?"

"No. Enjoy your food, she'll be all right."

It wasn't too much longer after that when the two of them got up. They shook hands like they had just completed a business deal. They walked off together, but she stopped at the bar while he left the restaurant.

"I'll be back."

"Want me to go with you, boss?" Kevon smiled and asked.

"No, I think I can mack a woman by myself."

I got up from the table and walked over to the bar. The woman smiled when she saw me coming. "Hello, Mr. Black. How are you?"

"I'm fine," I said and signed for the bartender. It was obvious that we had met before, but I still had no idea who this woman was or where I knew her from.

"Remy VSOP," I said to the bartender and turned to her.

"I thought it was you, but I wasn't sure. And I kept looking and looking. Your friend must have thought I was trying to flirt with him."

"He did."

"When you turned around I was sure it was you."

"You have me at a disadvantage."

"You don't remember me, do you?"

"I remember you, or I should say I recognize you. I just don't know from where."

She laughed. She had a pretty smile. "I'm not surprised. Even though the last time you saw me I was naked."

"You were?"

"Yes—I was."

I was really confused then. "If the last time I saw you, you were naked, I should at least remember your name."

"But you don't, do you?" she asked and continued to smile at me. She didn't seem the least bit angry that I didn't remember her name.

"No. I really don't remember your name, naked or not."

"That's because I probably never told you my name; at least not my real name."

"That makes me feel a little better."

She extended her name. "I'm Jada West."

"You're Jada West. I heard a lot about you."

"You have?" Jada smiled and laughed a little. "Well, I think I should be honored."

Jada West was slowly making a reputation for herself in some circles. She ran an agency for high-priced call girls. Simply put, Jada West was one of the top madams in the city. But by never being a client of hers or anybody that worked for her, that still didn't answer the question of where I knew her from.

"Like I said, I've heard a lot about you, so it's me who's honored to meet you. Or meet again."

"Let me stop messing with you. We met a couple of years ago at this little club called Ecstasy. They were having a private party for The One and his entourage and you were there. I was one of the dancers that night."

I looked at her a little closer. "I remember you, now," I said even though I didn't.

Jada gave me a look that told me that she knew I still didn't remember her. "We didn't talk for very long. You told me that you enjoyed watching me dance. I asked you if you were a friend of Bruce, Bruce. And you said that you owned the company that manages The One."

"Now I remember you," and this time I actually did. "I remember watching you dance. You were incredible."

Jada laughed. "I could do a little something back then."

"In fact, Bruce, Bruce invited me down there that night to see you; said you were the show."

"That was a long time ago."

"And I know why. I take it that this is much more profitable for you?"

"It is; and much easier on the feet."

I looked down. "And you have such pretty feet."

Jada giggled and I enjoyed the sound of it, and the smile that came with it. We talked at the bar over drinks for a while, mostly about the differences in our businesses. "Your clientele is primarily working class guys. Where my clientele is a bit more upscale," Jada said confidently. "My clients are doctors and lawyers, actors, directors and producers, executives, CEOs and politicians."

"Martin Marshall wouldn't be one of them?" I asked, always looking for any edge I could find.

"Martin, no, but I do know him. Martin Marshall is an arrogant, pompous jerk, but no, he's not a client," Jada said and looked at her watch. "Look at the time. I've gotta run." She reached in her purse and took out one of her cards. It only had a number on it. "It was good seeing you."

I accepted the card and kissed her hand. "Hopefully, it won't be the last time I see you."

"You have the card. It's my private number. Anything I

could do for you, just ask," Jada said and finished her drink.

"Before you go, let me ask you a question."

"Sure."

"Are any of your clients reporters?"

"Yes. Why do you ask?"

"Can you arrange a meeting?"

"With you?"

"No. I'm not sure who they'd be meeting with."

"As long as there's a story in it, I'm sure I can. His name is James Fremeno; he's a reporter for the *Post*. What's the story?"

I finished my drink and looked at Kevon. He stood up. "I'll call you in a couple of days."

"I'm sure that you will."

"Why is that?"

Jada smiled. "Because it seems that now I suddenly have something you want. And you impress me as a man who always gets what he wants."

"Not all the time."

What I really want is Cassandra.

But that's not gonna happen.

Chapter 34

Nick

I opened my eyes and looked around the room, halfway expecting Wanda to be sitting there watching me sleep.

It was after midnight by the time I got to Wanda's house. She was still up waiting for me when I got there. After I left Rain at the motel I thought it would be a good idea for me to be seen at a few of our spots. Since Wanda had eyes everywhere, I figured I'd put them to work for me.

"How'd it go?" Wanda asked as soon as I got in the house.

"Somebody got there before we did. They were dead when we got there."

"We? Who is we?"

"Me and Rain."

"Why you take her?"

"Wanda—we've been through this. Rain is helping me. We followed-up on her lead, then I dropped her off at J.R.'s."

"What you do after that?"

I laughed. "I really don't like being interrogated, counselor, but if you want me to account for my whereabouts, fine. After I dropped her off, I got a picture of her brother and then I went to Monika's. Then I hit a few spots." Wanda doesn't like Monika. She swears something is going on between us, so I know she won't call her for any reason.

"What you go to Monika's for?"

"She's helping me with Zakiya's murder, too. She was having an affair with a married man whose on-line name is Nice N. Slow. The e-mails were sent from a computer at J.R.'s. I think that Rain's brother Miles sent them. That's why I got his picture, so I could show it to the staff at Paradise tomorrow."

That was my plan for the day.

I got out of bed, took a shower, and was at Paradise by one. The place was packed. I made eye contact with Tasheka and took a seat. When things quieted down a little, Tasheka came to the table with some lemonade for me. "How are you doin', Nick?"

"I'm doin' fine, Tasheka. How about you?"

"Tired; need a better job. But other than that, I'm fine."

And she was; fine as hell.

"Have seat, Tasheka, I got something I want you to take a look at."

Tasheka sat down and I handed her the picture that I had taken of Miles. She looked at the picture and shook her head. "That's him. That's the guy she used to meet here."

"Are you sure?"

"Sure am," she said. "Shameka, come here."

"Don't you see I'm busy?" Shameka shouted back.

"I can't stand her ass sometimes," Tashekia frowned. "That's why I need a new job."

Tasheka got up. She took the pictures behind the counter to show Shameka. She looked at the pictures and came from behind the counter.

"That's him," Shameka said as soon as she got to the table.

"When they were here together, how did they act?"

"What do you mean?"

"Did they seem happy with each other? Did they argue?"

"They looked like they were in love. You know, sitting on the same side in the booth, all hugged up with each other. Holding hands, stuff like that."

She handed me back the pictures and asked if I was hungry. "Starvin'."

"What you want? You want some chicken, you want some fish?"

"Got any shrimp?"

"Of course. Some big jumbo joints."

"Bring me some shrimp and chicken."

"You want fries with that?"

"Hold the fries," I said and Shameka went for the food. Tasheka brought back the food and another glass of lemonade and sat down. While I ate, she told me all the reasons why she hated working there and needed to be gone.

"You got a pen?" I asked when I was finished eating. Tasheka went and got a pen and I wrote down the number for the finance company that Wanda had been dying for me to run. I handed it to her. "Call this number on Monday, but not until Monday. You ask for April Dancer, she'll be expecting your call," I said and got up.

Before I knew it, Tasheka had jumped up, hugged, and kissed me. "Thank you."

"Just don't disappoint me," I said, and could hear her scream for joy as I left the restaurant.

Now that I knew for sure that Miles was Nice N. Slow, the married man that Zakiya was seeing before her death, the question now was, what the fuck was I gonna do about it?

I had no idea.

When I got to J.R.'s it was still early, too early for the club to be open. I went around back and knocked on the door. A short time later a woman came to the door.

"I'm looking for Miles Robinson. Is he here?"

The woman took a closer look at me. "You were here with Rain yesterday, weren't you?"

"That's right."

"No, he's not," she said. "He won't be back until Monday."

"Thanks."

I went back around to the front of the building, thinking that now I had some time to decide what I was going to do about Miles. I was about to get in my car, when Rain pulled up in her BMW.

"Lookin' for me?" Rain asked as she pulled up alongside of me.

"No."

"Liar."

"No, I was looking for your brother, Miles."

"He ain't here."

"Yeah, I know. Some woman just told me that at the back door; said he won't be back until Monday."

"He dropped the kids off and took his wife out of town for the weekend, which ain't a bad idea. Why don't we go to AC for the weekend?"

"Not happenin', not this weekend, anyway." But it did sound good.

Rain put the car in park. "Since Miles ain't here, why don't you come ride with me for a minute?"

"Where you goin'?"

"Just ridin'."

I walked around to the other side of her car and got in. We drove around goin' nowhere fast, talkin' about nothing in particular. "There is something I always wanted to know," Rain said.

"What's that?"

"Did you and Freeze really set a nigga on fire?"

"What?"

"I heard that you and Freeze burned some nigga to death."

"We didn't burn him to death."

"So what happened?" Rain asked as she drove.

"The guy's name was Floyd Green. He worked at a garage and was runnin' a little numbers, but he made his money sellin' heroin. He owed André money. Black sent me and Freeze to get it."

"So far, that's how the story goes."

"As soon as he sees us, Floyd tries to run out the back door."

"But he trips on some tires. Y'all catch him, kick his ass, and set him on fire.

"That's not exactly what happened."

"I'm just sayin' that's how the story goes."

"Okay, here's what happened. Floyd trips on the tires and we started kickin' him. We're askin' him where the money is and he swears he ain't got it; he'll have it in a couple of days. Freeze picks up a tire and starts hitting him in the head with it. I pulled him up and tell Freeze to put the tire around him."

"That's when y'all set him on fire."

"You gonna let me tell this?"

"Go ahead. But I'm still waitin' for this to be any different from what I heard," Rain laughed.

"You wanna hear this or not?"

"Go on. You know you wanna tell me," Rain said in a voice that made me want to be inside her.

"After Freeze put the tire around him, we took our time

and worked him over. He still kept sayin' that he would have the money in a couple of days. I was ready to leave it at that, but to make sure he understood that I was serious, I told Freeze to find me some gasoline. I poured it around the tire and asked Freeze for a lighter. Before I lit it, Floyd tells me the money is in the safe. He took us to the safe, told me the combination and got us our money."

Rain laughed. "Right. That's when y'all niggas set his ass on fire and he burned to death."

"No, we didn't set him on fire. After that Floyd left the city. I heard he moved to Philly, but we didn't set him on fire," I said as Rain pulled into the motel she'd been staying at.

Rain unlocked the door and we went inside. Apparently, she had gone by her apartment after I left her. She had clothes everywhere, some were hung up, and some were on the second bed in the room.

"Planning on being here for a while?"

"No, I just ain't goin' back to my apartment. I need to be findin' a place, but I ain't feelin' it right now."

"What you feelin' like right now."

Rain pulled her top over her head and unbuttoned her pants. I figured out the rest.

Before too long I was naked and laying across the bed. Rain straddled me and eased herself down on me. She rode me slowly while she sucked her nipple. I began to feel her legs trembling on my thighs and I pumped a little harder. Rain reached out and touched my face with her hands and kissed me.

Rain stood up and then kneeled down on the edge of the bed. I put my hands on her hips and entered her slowly. No matter how hard I tried, I couldn't get the image of Wanda out of my mind. *What was I doing?* I thought while I continued to slide in and out of her.

Her cell rang, but she didn't choose to answer it.

Rain rolled over and I eased her on her back and entered her. Her body began to quiver as she stretched out her legs.

The cell ran again, but this time as soon as it stopped the room phone started ringing. "Shit!" Rain yelled and pushed me off of her. "This better be important," she said and answered the phone. "This better be fuckin' important!" Rain yelled into the phone.

"What?" She said and stood up. "When?" I sat and watched as Rain held the phone and listened. I watched her facial expression change from anger to pain. A look of panic washed over her face and she looked around the room. "I'll be there as soon as I can," Rain said and hung up the phone.

"What?"

"That was Jeff Ritchie. Pops had a heart attack."

Chapter 35

Rain was too shook-up to do anything, so I drove her to the hospital. When we got there, Jeff Ritchie told her that J.R. was in his office at the club, having a steak, and he suddenly grabbed his chest and fell to his knees. "He's in intensive care. They don't know if he's gonna make it. You can go in," he told her.

"You call Miles?"

"He's on his way back. He'll be here in a few hours."

Good. Now I don't have to wait until Monday.

Rain turned to me. "I'm gonna go in and see my father. Don't leave me, Nick, okay. Don't leave."

Rain grabbed the first nurse she could find and they took her to the intensive care unit. Jeff Ritchie looked at me and I looked at him with a *yeah, I fucked her* look on my face. He shook his head and walked away. I went in the waiting room and sat down.

I had been sitting there people-watching, 'cause it was more entertaining than television, for over an hour before Rain came back and sat down next to me. It was obvious that she had been crying, so I put my arm around her. I held her for a while before she spoke.

"The doctor said his main coronary artery was completely blocked and the other two was just about blocked. They did bypass surgery on him."

"Is he gonna be all right?"

"They don't know. Said we just have to wait and see. Look, I'm gonna go back in there. You can go if you want to."

"You go ahead and be with your father. I'm gonna stay for a while," I said knowing that I wanted to talk to Miles, but thinking that maybe this wasn't the best time to hit him with this.

"You sure?"

"Yeah, I'm cool. You go ahead."

Rain went back in the unit and I reclaimed my seat. It was two hours later when I looked up and saw Miles and Lakeda go in the unit. It would be another hour before Rain came out again. "He regained consciousness. He's still very weak, but they say he has a good chance."

"That's good to know. I'm gonna go ahead and leave," I said and handed her, her keys. I had decided that I would wait and talk to Miles another time. "I'll take a cab back to my car."

"Thanks for stayin' as long as you did. I'll call you tomorrow." Rain kissed me on the cheek and walked back toward the unit. I watched her until the door closed behind her.

I caught a cab back to my car and went and hit a few of our spots. As I went from spot to spot, I wondered who Wanda's spies were and how I was gonna find out who they were. Maybe she was clocking me right now.

I thought about what Black said about not hurting Wanda. It wasn't like I was trying to hurt her, but I knew that I was. Even if Wanda didn't know for sure that I was fuckin' Rain, every minute I spent with her, every time I'm with Wanda and I think about Rain, I was driving the knife a little deeper. I loved Wanda, but there was something about Rain, something I wasn't ready to give up.

I called Wanda and told her that I was gonna make a few more stops and then I would be there. "That's if you want to see me," I said.

"Of course I want to see you. How long do you think you'll be?"

"I don't know."

My next stop for the night was the game. I stayed there for awhile and talked to Jackie. "Where's Travis tonight?"

"Monika called him last night, and he rushed out of here. I haven't seen him since," Jackie told me.

"What's up with that?"

"I don't know. Maybe Monika had a tip on a hot job and needed Travis for it. You know how they roll."

"Yeah, she did say she was into something the last time I talked to her."

When I left Jackie, I decided to call it a night and head for Wanda's, but I called Rain first to check on her. "Where you at?"

"On my way home."

"Your home or your woman's?"

"Hers."

"Tell her I said hello."

"No."

"Why don't you stop by here on your way? I promise not to keep you too long." I started to tell her no. "I just need you to hold me for awhile," Rain said, and against my better judgment, I agreed.

I drove back to the hospital thinking of how just about every time Rain and I were together we killed somebody.

Now she needed a hug. Under all that gangster—Go figure.

When I got back to the hospital, I didn't see Rain anywhere, so I was about to go in visitor's area to wait for her. I saw Jeff Ritchie sitting there and then I saw Miles come out of the intensive care unit and walk down the hall. Since the old man was gonna be all right, I thought I might catch Miles weak and he'd actually tell me the truth.

I followed Miles to the cafeteria. He got a cup of coffee from the vending machine and sat down at one of the tables. I waited a minute before I went and joined him. When I sat down, Miles didn't seem to notice that I was there. Then he looked at me. "You're Nick, right? Rain's friend?"

"Yes. Sorry about your father. Is he going to be all right?"

"I don't know. He's awake now. His arteries are so blocked that it's restricting the flow of blood. He may be in danger of having a stroke. They say we'll have to wait and see."

"This might not be the best time, but I need to ask you something."

"What's that?"

I took Zakiya's picture out of my pocket and slid it in front of him. "You wanna tell me about her?"

"I told you that I didn't know her," Miles said and started to get up.

"Yes, you do. You were having an affair with her. Nice N. Slow? That's you, right?"

Then Miles did something that I really wasn't expecting him to do.

He started crying.

I mean crying-like-a-baby crying.

I felt like shit for asking.

"I loved her," Miles said and picked up Zakiya's picture and stared at it.

"What happened?"

"I met her at the club a year ago. She was there to meet somebody, but he stood her up. And I wondered what kind of fool would stand up somebody as beautiful and sweet as her."

"How long after that did the affair begin?"

"That night." Miles looked up at me. "I loved her from that first minute I saw her. I know it was wrong. I have a beautiful wife, two wonderful kids. I know everything about what I was feeling for Zakiya was wrong. But I couldn't help myself. It was like nothing mattered to me except being with Zakiya. But it was wrong and I knew it had to end."

"So you had her killed?"

"What? What are you talking about? She was killed during a robbery."

"You hired those two men to kill her. The robbery was just a front."

"I didn't have her killed. You've gotta believe me. I loved her!"

"They walked right up to her and killed her."

"No," Miles insisted. "It was a robbery. The police said it was some type of gang thing, I don't know, but I didn't have anything to do with it. Don't you understand; I couldn't hurt her. She was—too important to me."

"No, Miles, you hired those men and they shot her."

"That's not true. I don't believe you!" Miles said and jumped up.

"Come with me," I said and stood up too.

"Where are we going?"

"To watch a murder."

Miles and I walked through the hospital and passed

Jeff Ritchie still sitting in the visitor's area. Along the way, I thought what if I'm wrong? What if he's telling the truth, and he really didn't have anything to do with it?

When we got outside, he followed me to my car and we got in. I took the DVD of the murder out of the glove compartment and put it in DVD player. "Watch for yourself."

I sat and looked at Miles while he watched the video; saw the smile come over his face when he saw Zakiya, and then I watched him breakdown when he saw her die.

I felt like shit.

"I wouldn't," he said through his tears. "I couldn't. She was going to have a baby." Miles looked at me. "Our baby. I was meeting her there that day to tell her that I would stand by her; that I would take care of her and our baby."

"Who else knew she would be there that day?"

"Nobody," Miles said quickly and then he looked at me. "Lakeda knew."

"How did she find out?"

"That night before, I was in the office and Zakiya called. I knew Lakeda was in the club, so I told her that I couldn't talk and would see her at Paradise tomorrow. I didn't hear Lakeda when she came in. I don't know how long she was there before I noticed her, but she heard enough. She heard me tell Zakiya that I loved her."

"What happened after that?"

"We argued about it. A lot of 'how could you?' and 'how long has it been going on?' kind of stuff. Then she left and she didn't get home until after midnight. I asked her where she'd been, but we just started arguing about Zakiya again, so I went and slept on the couch."

"You think she had her killed? Does she have that kind of juice to have somebody killed?"

"I don't know."

Miles got out of the car and went back in the hospital.

Chapter 36

I let Miles get a bit of a head start before I followed him in the hospital. It wasn't like I didn't know where he was going. Miles was going to confront his wife about his dead mistress.

Ballsy; I'd give him that.

Did Lakeda really have Zakiya killed? I didn't know much about her, but from what I saw I didn't think she had it in her. But you never know how far a woman, or a man for that matter, will go in the name of love.

I, on the other hand, knew. I had no illusions about what Wanda was capable of, and what she'd do if she knew for sure what I was doing with Rain. Wanda could and would have Rain killed. It only served to remind me of what a dangerous game I was playing.

Miles went back to the unit. I couldn't follow him, so I took a seat in the visitor's area. I looked around for Jeff Ritchie, but didn't see him. It didn't take long for Miles to come bursting out of the intensive care unit dragging Lakeda behind him. Rain came rushing out behind them.

I got up and caught up with Rain as she rushed to catch

up with Miles and Lakeda. "What's goin' on?" I asked, even though I knew.

"I don't know. Miles busted in the room and pulled Lakeda up from her chair and said 'I wanna talk to you.' "

We followed them out into the parking lot and caught up with them just as the show began.

Miles stopped and grabbed Lakeda by the shoulders and shook her. "What did you do?"

"Nothing. I didn't do anything!" Lakeda yelled back.

"What did you do?" Miles screamed again and continued shaking Lakeda.

"Stop it, Miles. What the fuck is wrong with you?" Rain yelled.

"Stay out of this, Rain! This has nothing to do with you!" Miles yelled at his sister.

"Tell me what you did!" Miles yelled at Lakeda.

Rain took a step toward Miles like she wanted to try and separate them, but I stopped her. "Leave him alone."

Rain looked down at my hand on her arm and snatched it back. "You did this, didn't you? What did you tell him?"

"The truth."

"What truth?"

"Miles was having an affair was Zakiya Phillips."

"The chick that got killed at your spot?"

"Miles thinks Lakeda sent those men to kill her." Rain looked at me like she didn't or couldn't believe what I was telling her. And then she looked at her brother; saw the fury in his eyes. "He was in love with her."

"I don't know what you're talking about, Miles," Lakeda insisted.

"Don't lie to me!"

"Stop it, Miles, you're hurting me."

"Then tell me what you did."

"What are you talking about?"

"About Zakiya."

"What about her?" Lakeda asked. She looked confused by his question. Like she really didn't know what he was talking about.

"You knew about her. You were the only one who knew about us and you had her killed."

"I don't know what you're talking about. I didn't have that bitch killed. I didn't even know she was dead."

"Don't lie to me Lakeda! It was you! After you heard me say that I loved her, you got somebody to kill her."

"Damn, Miles, you told her that shit?" Rain said, but I'm sure Miles didn't hear her.

By that time a small crowd had joined us to watch the show. There's nothing more entertaining than black folks fightin' in public.

"Let me go, Miles," Lakeda said and suddenly found the strength to break away from Miles. Probably that line about loving another woman gave her strength. "I didn't have her killed. I wish I did and I'm glad that bitch is dead, but I didn't get anybody to kill her."

"You knew I was going to meet her that day. You knew where I was meeting her!" Miles grabbed her again and Lakeda struggled to get free.

"Let me go!"

"Tell me what you did!" Miles yelled and slapped the shit outta her. I grabbed Miles and held him before he could slap her again. Rain rushed to Lakeda's side and held her. Miles began to cry to again. "Just tell me what you did."

"Okay, people. Show's over," I said and walked Miles away from the crowd. Rain followed with Lakeda. Once we were far enough from the slowly dispersing crowd I stopped, but I kept my hands on Miles just in case he decided to go at her again.

"Where did you go after you left that night?" I asked Lakeda.

"All right." Lakeda pushed Rain off her. "All right." Lakeda was breathing hard and took a second to compose herself. "I drove around for awhile and then went back to the club looking for her. I was gonna make her leave you alone."

"Was she there?"

"No."

"What did you do then?"

"I had a few drinks and I came home," Lakeda said, and then the look on her face changed.

"What?" I asked.

"What did you do!" Miles demanded to know.

"I talked to Jeff Ritchie."

"What did you tell him?" I asked.

"I needed somebody to talk to. So I told him about the affair. Told him that you said you loved her."

"But I told you that I would never leave you and the kids, Lakeda. I told you that."

"I know what you told me, Miles. But I was mad that night; mad enough to kill you, not her, Miles, you. That's why I left."

"What did you tell Jeff Ritchie?" I asked.

"I told him that Miles said he was meeting her at that restaurant. I told him that I was going to be there, too."

"What did he say?"

"He said that I should go home and be with my husband. That he knew how these things were, and when you realized what you had and what you had to lose, that you would come to your senses and leave her alone."

"Let me go," Miles said calmly and I did what he asked. He walked up to Lakeda and slowly reached for her hand.

"I didn't have her killed, Miles." Now it's Lakeda who began to shed tears.

"I know. Don't cry, Lakeda. It wasn't your fault. This is

all my fault. I should never have let that happen. Never did that to you."

"I didn't deserve that, Miles. Do you know how hard it was for me to hear you say 'I love you' to another woman?"

"Yes, and I'm sorry that I hurt you, I swear, nothing like that will ever happen again. I only hope that you can forgive me."

"I don't know, Miles. I'm trying, you know that, but it's going to take time for me to get past this."

"Please, Lakeda, just say that you forgive me."

"I forgive you, Miles, but I meant what I said. It's just gonna take some time."

Miles put his arms around Lakeda and hugged her. Slowly, Lakeda put her arms around him. "Let's go back inside and see about Pops."

"That's not right," Rain said, and we all started walking back toward the building, but I knew it wasn't over.

Once we were back inside, Miles saw Jeff Ritchie going back in the visitor's area and he took-off running. Rain went running after him. "Miles!"

I looked at Lakeda before I started to run. She smiled at me and kept walking at the same pace. I knew then there was more to this then she had said.

Miles ran up to Jeff Ritchie and hit him in the face and the two men began wrestling until me and Rain got there to separate them. "You killed her, didn't you?" Miles said as I dragged him away from Jeff Ritchie. "You fuckin' bastard, you killed her."

"What are you talking about, Miles? And lower your voice," Jeff Ritchie said as hospital staff began to take notice of us.

"Let's take this outside," I suggested.

"No, Nick, let me go. I'm all right."

Since he appeared to be calm enough, I let Miles go. He walked up to Jeff Ritchie and got in his face. "I know what you did," Miles said quietly. "I know you had Zakiya killed. It couldn't have been anybody but you. The family protector; the man who makes things right."

Lakeda finally caught up to us and Miles turned and looked at her. "Lakeda told you everything. She told you who Zakiya was and where she was gonna be, and you sent two men to kill her."

"I'm sorry, Miles," Jeff Ritchie said. "It wasn't supposed to be like this."

"Like what? Wasn't supposed to be like what? I wasn't supposed to find out, is that it?"

Jeff Ritchie shook his head. "I only did what had to be done."

Miles nodded his head and backed away from him slowly. "Yeah, me too." He turned and walked away from the area. Rain started to go after him. "Leave me alone, Rain."

"Where you goin'?"

"I need some air," Miles said and kept walking.

Rain stopped and watched as her brother left the building.

Jeff Ritchie looked at me like he wanted to do something. "Come on with it," I said softly.

"Me and you will settle this another time," Jeff Ritchie said to me. Then he went and sat down.

Rain walked up and stood by me. "Something ain't right about this."

"What do you mean?"

"I'll tell you later," Rain said. "I'm goin' to check on Pops. Why don't you go check on Miles and then go on and get outta here. And call me tomorrow."

"I will," I said and started to leave when I saw Miles coming toward us.

Miles walked by Rain and I calmly. "You okay?" Rain asked as he passed.

"I'm fine, Rain, you go check on Pops," Miles said and went back in the visitor's area. Miles walked up to Jeff Ritchie and stood over him. When Jeff Ritchie looked up, Miles took the gun out of his pocket and pointed it at him.

"Miles, no!" Rain yelled and we rushed at him.

"She was having my baby!" Miles yelled and put three shots in Jeff Ritchie's chest and one to the head.

Miles let the gun drop to the floor and sat down in the chair next to Jeff Ritchie. Lakeda sat down next to him. She took his hand in hers and tears rolled down her cheeks. Doctors and nurses flooded into the room and tried to save Jeff Ritchie, but he was dead.

Miles didn't offer any resistance when the police and hospital security arrived on the scene. Miles stood up and put his hands behind his back.

I stood there with Rain, watching as they took Miles away. Then she turned to me. "Something ain't right about this."

"What?"

"Come on." Rain took me by the hand and we walked toward the intensive care unit. She told the attendant that I was her husband and they let me go in with her.

We went in J.R.'s room and Rain sat down next to him. She took his hand. "The police just took Miles to jail for killing Jeff Ritchie."

"What?" J.R. said in barely a whisper. "Why?"

"Lakeda found out that Miles was having an affair. She said she told Jeff Ritchie and he sent the men that killed the woman."

J.R. closed his eyes and turned away from Rain.

"But something ain't right about her story. Lakeda wouldn't talk to Jeff Ritchie about Miles having an affair. But she would talk you. Lakeda came to see you that night. That's what happened, ain't it, Daddy?"

J.R. didn't answer, didn't open his eyes; he just gripped Rain's hand a little tighter.

"Jeff Ritchie would never do anything like that. He wouldn't send men to kill her, not unless you told him to."

Rain let go of her father's hand and stood up.

J.R. opened his eyes.

"She was pregnant with Miles's baby, Daddy. You killed your grandchild."

When Rain walked out of the room, J.R. looked at me. I thought about what Black said.

If J.R.'s involved, kill him.

"You shouldn't have hit her at our spot, J.R."

"Didn't know it was your spot."

"Guess not," I said and walked out of the room.

Chapter 37

Mike Black

It took a couple of days for me think through what I was gonna do, and a week to put it all together. But I was almost ready to put my plan into action. There was just one more piece that I needed to put in place—the most important piece.

Kevon parked the car and we went in the building. We took the elevator up and Kevon knocked on the door.

"Who is it?"

I leaned in front of the peephole. "Mike Black."

"Don't go nowhere. I gotta put something on."

"Don't go to any trouble."

"Maybe you should call first, boss," Kevon said and leaned against the wall. I took the other wall and we waited.

Five minutes later the door opened. "Hello, Mr. Black," CeCe said. I don't know what she had on before, but now she looked radiant. Knowing my fondness for the color, CeCe was wearing a black dress and four-inch stilettos, her hair was done, and her make-up was flawless.

"I didn't catch you at a bad time, did I?"

"Not at all. I was just sitting around watching TV. Please come in," CeCe said and extended her hand gracefully. I walked in and CeCe looked at Kevon. "He's not coming in?"

"He'll be right there if I need him."

"I understand." CeCe smiled and shut the door.

I followed her into the living room and she offered me a seat. "Nice place," I said and sat down.

"Thank you," CeCe said and sat down next to me. "It would be an understatement to say that I'm surprised to see you. I didn't know you knew where I lived. But you did say that when you wanted me, you would find me."

"Sorry I didn't call first, but I needed to talk to you about somethin' and I don't like talkin' on telephones."

"I heard that about you. That's why I haven't blown-up Kevon's phone."

"I appreciate that."

"So, what do I owe the honor of this visit?"

"I need you to do something very important for me."

"You know I'll do anything for you. Just tell me what you need?"

"I arranged for you to meet with a reporter from the *Post*."

CeCe frowned. "For what?"

"I want you to give him a story."

CeCe looked at me for a second or two and then she sat back. "This is about your wife, ain't it?"

"Yes."

"I thought so."

"What you know about my wife?"

"I know that she was murdered, and that they accused you of her murder. I know that finding her killers is the only thing that's important to you."

"You've been talkin' to Bobby."

CeCe smiled. "I know a lot more about her, but you don't wanna hear all that."

"Try me."

"I know that you loved her very much."

"I still do."

"Is she what keeps you from letting me get close to you?"

I didn't answer her because she was right. I won't let anybody get close to me. I didn't want to feel for any other woman what I felt for Cassandra. But there was something about CeCe.

"I guess that answers my question," CeCe said and got up. She stood over me and shook her head.

I wanted to tell her how beautiful she looked standing over me like that, but I didn't. I had to admit that her appeal to me is much more than physical. The thing was that I liked CeCe. Liked her look, liked her style, liked the way she handled herself.

CeCe stood there looking at me, and then she walked away. "I'll do what you need me to do for you, but after I do it, there's something I want you to do for me."

"What's that?"

"Do we have a deal?"

"You haven't told me what you want."

"Do we have a deal, Mr. Black?"

"Not until you tell me what you want."

"Believe me, it's nothing you can't do."

"Then why can't you just tell me," I laughed.

"Do we have a deal?" CeCe came and sat next to me again. "Look, you want me to do something for you. I want you to do something for me. Since you're sitting here I know it's something important to you, or you wouldn't be here. Bottom line, you *need* me. When I'm done doing whatever it is that you *need* me to do for you,

I *need* you to do something for me. So do we have a deal, Mr. Black?" CeCe said for the fourth time and extended her hand.

Once again, I knew that CeCe was right. I did need her and it was something that only she could do. I accepted her hand. "Deal."

"Good. So what can I do for you?"

I stood up and extended my hand. "Come with me."

"Where are we going, handsome?"

"To meet some people."

We left CeCe's apartment and Kevon drove us to Monika's. Since she already knew about Cassandra's murder I told CeCe that Vinnelli had arranged the murder, and that he was our target. When we arrived Monika opened the door and let us in. "CeCe, this is Monika Wynn and Travis Burns."

"Hey," Monika said half-heartedly.

Travis got up and shook her hand. "Nice to meet you, CeCe."

"Good to meet you both," CeCe said and looked at Monika.

"Now that we're all here." I went and sat down next to CeCe. "I'll tell you why we're here and your part in it. I intend to destroy Agent Vinnelli. Over the last few weeks Monika has been compiling information on Vinnelli that you're gonna feed to the press."

"Why me?"

"Because your past relationship with Steven 'Cash Money' Blake gives the story credibility. And it's something that he can verify with the police."

"What about him?"

"Nothing really, but he connects to Mylo, or as you know him, the late agent Clint Harris. He connects to the late Agent Masters." Monika put a picture of Mylo and Masters in front of her. "And Masters connects to Vinnelli."

"Okay," CeCe said, but I knew it still wasn't clear to her.

"You're gonna tell the reporter about Mylo's dealings with Cash. Then you're gonna give him information about a meeting between Mylo and Masters discussing several murders, and taking over drug markets. Then you'll give him the head man, Vinnelli, and information about his offshore accounts. That's just the first part of the plan."

I got up and stood by Travis. I looked at Monika. "How much is in those accounts?"

"Right now there's $7,562,753 in those accounts. It will be more allowing for interest earned between now and when we make our move."

"Thank you. Now, when that information becomes public, the government will freeze those accounts, but not before we take half of it."

"Why just half?" CeCe asked.

"Because I want the government to have something to freeze. Monika, half is how much?"

"Roughly $3,781,376."

"Which we split four ways. And that is?"

"That's $945,345—each," Monika added.

"Any questions?"

CeCe's jaw dropped and we all laughed at her.

"Welcome to the big time," Monika said to CeCe.

"You still want me to do something for you?" I asked, thinking that damn near a million dollars would be enough compensation for her part in my plan.

"Yes," CeCe said definitely. "And a deal's a deal. But I do have a question."

"What's that?"

"What if the reporter doesn't believe me? I mean, that's gonna be a lot to remember."

"I'll coach you on what you need to say," Monika assured CeCe. "And when you talk to him, you'll be wearing a wire and an ear piece. Me and Black will be someplace close by listening and we'll help keep you straight."

"You in?"

"I already told you yes, and a deal's a deals," CeCe said.

"Travis. The money—"

"Like Black said, the money is in offshore accounts in different banks. So we can't just roll in there and take it at gunpoint. In order for us to get it, I gotta access the network and get past a 128-bit encryption. Now accessing the secure cluster has to be done on a computer at a bank on the backbone of the network. I have a friend who works in investment and special services at a bank in the Cayman Islands, which is part of the network.

"By placing a packet sniffer on a network I can capture and analyze all of the network traffic. Then I use a hydra which, for lack of a better definition, is a log-in cracker. I go in, pop the firewall, drop in the hydra and transfer the money into another account."

The next morning Travis left for the Cayman Islands to wait for my call.

For the next two days, Monika and I drilled CeCe on what she would say to the reporter. By the end of the second day she was ready. I was impressed, but I knew I would be. There is much more to her appeal than the physical.

That night CeCe met the reporter at One if by Land, Two if by Sea, a restaurant on Barrow and West 4th Streets. Monika and I were seated at a table near the one where *New York Post* reporter James Fremeno waited for her to arrive.

After Monika did a sound check on the equipment, CeCe went in. "Mr. Fremeno?"

Fremeno sprang to his feet when he saw CeCe coming. "I'm Cameisha Collins. Sorry I'm late. I hope I didn't keep you waiting long?"

"Not at all, Ms. Collins. Please have a seat."

"Thank you."

"Now, tell me what I can do for you?"

"Well, a few months ago my boyfriend Steven was murdered in my apartment."

"I'm sorry to hear that. Do you know who did it?"

"DEA agents."

"That's a very serious accusation, Ms. Collins. Do you have any proof that it was the DEA?"

"Yes, I do. My boyfriend Steven was a drug dealer who went by the name Cash Money."

"I understand."

"Do you remember a couple of months ago a DEA agent was killed at a parking garage and a few days later, another agent was found dead at his house outside of Philadelphia?"

"Vaguely."

CeCe took out the pictures we gave her and pushed them in front of Fremeno. "That's them," she said, and told Fremeno about the meeting. For the next half-hour, Fremeno took notes and sat fascinated by the story CeCe was telling to him.

When she was done with her story, CeCe made one request. "I know that you need to verify what I told you, but before you go to print with the story, I know you have to call the DEA to ask if they want to comment on the story."

"That's right. It's more of a courtesy than a requirement, but yes."

"All I ask is that before you do that you call me."

"I can do that," Fremeno readily agreed.

It was two weeks later when CeCe got the call from Fremeno. As soon as she hung up with him, CeCe called Kevon and he handed the phone to me. "It's on."

"Thank you." I hung and called Travis. "It's on."

The story hit the paper that next morning.

Chapter 38

I sat in my office at Cuisine that next morning and read the paper. Fremeno had written a very interesting article that took his readers step-by-step through Cash Money's murder to Mylo and his meeting with Masters, and dropped the whole thing on Vinnelli, just the way I planned.

I looked at my watch. It was ten-thirty. If FedEx was as good as their word, Mrs. Vinnelli should have pictures of her husband with Eileen McManus, and details of their affair. Eileen McManus, on the other hand, should have pictures of Vinnelli with Pamela Connote. That by itself was enough to wreck his world, but it would be just the beginning.

Kevon came to the table with the phone in his hand. "It's Travis."

"Good morning, Travis. Tell me something positive."

"I just left the bank with a check made out the way you asked, for three million, eight hundred thousand dollars."

"Now that's positive. Any problems?"

"None."

"You take care of your people?"

"Yes, sir," Travis said. I gave him a quarter of a million dollars to give his contact for her part in the plan. "I'm on my way to the airport now, so I'll see you this afternoon."

"Good man. I'll have your money waiting for you when you get here."

When Travis got back, I would have a million dollars in cash ready for him. I told Nick to find somebody else to baby-sit Jackie at the game. I could use Travis for other things on both sides of the house. Him and Monika were going to be very valuable people to have around.

When I hung up the phone Kevon came back in the office. "You never guess who is here to see you, boss."

"Martin Marshall."

Kevon looked at his watch. "More than an hour before you say he be here."

"Show him in."

A few minutes later Martin was shutting the door to my office. You know, for some reason, he didn't look happy. He walked up to the desk and saw the paper.

"That your doing?"

"I don't know what you're talkin' about, Martin. Have a seat. Can I get you a drink?"

"Whiskey."

"How do you take it?" I asked and got up to fix us both a drink.

"In a glass." Martin picked up the paper from my desk and started mumbling as he looked at it.

"Here you go, Martin." I handed him his glass and sat down.

Martin dropped the paper on the desk and leaned forward. "Fremeno could have only gotten this stuff from you," he said and pointed to the article. "When I gave you that name I thought you would just take his money and kill him, not go running to the press with it." Martin sat back in his chair. "When they start digging into this, Vinnelli will flip on me if it comes down to it."

"You'll be all right, Martin. I hear you're Teflon. Nothing sticks to you. And besides, Vinnelli is gonna be too busy with his own issues to even remember your name."

"I'm running for congress, Black. He's gonna remember my name."

"Don't comment on it, or make some bullshit statement supporting the integrity of the DEA. Ain't that what you politicians do?"

"I don't need you to tell me how to handle the press. The fact is that I trusted you, and you fucked me."

"I didn't fuck you, Martin. If I wanted to fuck you, Martin, I would have given them this." I picked up the remote and turned on the recording of Martin's conversation with Diego Estaban.

When it was over, I handed him the Justice Department memo that Monika uncovered. "And I would have given them that."

"Where did you get this?" Martin asked as he continued looking at the memo.

"Like you said, Martin, my people are very talented." When Martin looked up, I had my gun pointed at him. "I should kill you right now, Martin. If for nothing else, for your part in Diego's plan."

"That was just business," Martin said putting his hands up.

"That's the only reason you're still alive. I understand that it was just business. That—and the fact that we can do things for each other in the future. And put your hands down." Martin put his hands down slowly. "I just needed for us to have an understanding."

"What understanding is that?"

"That you don't fuck with me."

There was a knock at the door and Kevon stuck his head in. "Nick is here, boss."

"I have a meeting to go to, Martin," I said and stood up. "So, if we're done here . . ."

Martin stood up and I extended my hand. "Don't worry, I'm not done with Vinnelli," I said quietly and shook his hand.

After Martin left, Kevon drove me and Nick out to Yonkers to see Angelo. I had been putting him off for weeks. Now that this Vinnelli business was over, it was time to move forward.

When we got to the social club, I was surprised that Fat Jimmy didn't meet us at the car, so I asked Angee when we got inside, "Where's fat Jimmy? He sick or something?"

"Jimmy's dead, Mikey. His wife caught him with another broad and shot them both."

"That's fucked up."

"It is that. So, Mikey, you been thinkin' about what I asked you?"

"I have. I thought a lot about it, but for personal reasons that I know you understand, I'm gonna have to say no."

"That's unfortunate, but not unexpected."

"Before you decide to whack me hear me out, Angee."

"I'm not gonna have you whacked, Mikey."

"That's good to know. Like I said, Angee, I can't get involved for my own reasons, but what I will do as a personal favor to you, is I will offer advice and counsel to Stark, and should the need ever arise, I'll act as an intermediary to resolve any disputes. You got a problem with him, you come to me. But understand, this is not a service. This I do for you out of friendship. I will not accept a fee. But for reasons that I know you understand, I can't go any further than that."

"You know what? That means a lot to me. It does, Mikey. I expected you to say no just like you did. I knew I was askin' a lot of you, and if you had said yes, I knew it wouldn't be because you wanted to or because of the money or because it was good business. None of that. If you had said yes to this it would be out of loyalty to our friendship. But this—" Angee stood up with his arms out.

I stood up. "I hope that's acceptable." Angee came around table and hugged me. Then he kissed me on both cheeks and held my face in both hands. I thought the kiss of death was coming next.

"This means a lot to me, Mikey," he said and we left his office. When we came out, Nick and Kevon stood up. Angee walked over and shook Nick's hand. "Congratulations, Nick, you deserve it."

"Thank you," Nick said.

I had Kevon drop Nick back at the club. When he left I had one more stop to make. After Kevon parked the car, I got a briefcase out of the trunk and we went in the building. We took the elevator up and Kevon knocked on the door.

"Who is it?"

I leaned in front of the peephole. "Mike Black."

"Don't go nowhere. I gotta put something on."

"Don't go to any trouble."

"I tell you again, maybe you should call first, boss," Kevon said and leaned against the wall. I took the other wall and once again, we waited. Five minutes later CeCe opened the door.

"Hello, Mr. Black."

"Hello, CeCe. I'm not interrupting anything, am I?"

"Not at all. Please come in. But you could think about calling first."

"Kevon said the same thing," I said and sat down.

"So, I read the paper this morning. I hope you're pleased?" CeCe sat down next to me.

"I am." I put the briefcase on the coffee table in front of her.

"Is that for me?"

I nodded my head.

CeCe opened the case, looked at the money, and closed the case.

"I hope you're pleased?"

"I am." CeCe put the briefcase on the floor next to her. "This must mean that everything went all right in the Caymans, and that I satisfied my end of the deal?"

"It does."

"So are you ready to live up to your end of the deal?"

"As soon as you tell me what it is."

"I want you to take me to dinner and then I want you to take me dancing," CeCe said.

"That's it? Dinner and dancing?"

"That's it, Mr. Black, dinner and dancing."

"Let's go."

"No, not tonight. I want you to make reservations at some place nice. It can be vegetarian, I don't mind that."

"You have been talkin' to Bobby."

"Bobby likes to talk to me," CeCe said and smiled. "After you make reservations, I want you to call me and let me know what time to be ready."

"That's it? Dinner and dancing?"

"That's all I want," CeCe said and showed me to the door.

I called her the next day and told her that we had dinner reservations for six that evening and that I would pick her up at five-thirty. I arrived on time and CeCe was ready as I expected by six. She looked fantastic.

We had dinner reservations at Le Bernardin on 51st

Street between 6th and 7th Avenue. CeCe had baked shrimp and striped bass and I ordered the sautéed codfish and we talked. Something she and I hadn't done a lot of. "Because you avoid me."

"I don't avoid you, I'm just busy."

"I'm busy, too, I have a lot to do to get this store opened, but I seem to find time for the things I want."

"How's that goin'?"

"It's been a little rough. That briefcase you handed me will make things a lot easier. I should be able to open on time."

"I meant to ask you when you first told me about it, but what do you know about running a store?"

"I used to be a buyer for Nostrums in Seattle."

"Really?"

"You seem surprised. What did you think I was gonna say; that I used to be a cashier at Macys?"

I laughed, but yeah, I did.

"Well, I was a cashier at Macys, too, but I used to be a buyer."

"I didn't know that about you."

CeCe looked at me like I was stupid. "There's a lot that you don't know about me, Mr. Black."

"You're right."

"And I want you to know me. I want you to know that I'm more than just some gold-diggin' baller's girlfriend."

By the time the waiter brought the check I knew that her real name was Cameisha Collins. She graduated from The University of Bridgeport with a degree in fashion merchandising. She moved to Seattle and worked for Nostrums out of their corporate office as a buyer. She came back to New York when her mother got sick. When she couldn't find a job as a buyer, she got the job as a cashier at Macys and that's where she met Cash Money. "You know the rest of the story."

I had found out something else about CeCe. I found that I liked her. I've always enjoyed the company of women who could hold a conversation, and CeCe was definitely one of those women. She was intelligent without being snotty about it; she was playful, but not silly. CeCe was flirtatious, but not necessarily sexual.

And she was beautiful to look at.

"What now?" CeCe asked as we walked out of the restaurant arm in arm. "It's a little early to go dancing."

"I know it wasn't part of our deal, but if you'd like, I got tickets for *Cat on a Hot Tin Roof*: the new production of the Tennessee Williams' classic with an all-black cast."

"How did you know I wanted to see that play?"

"I didn't."

"Well, Mr. Black, I would like that very much."

"It's playing at The Broadhurst Theatre on West 44th Street," I said as Kevon arrived with the car.

After the play was over we went dancing, and I gotta say, although *Cat on a Hot Tin Roof* was great, watching CeCe dance was the highlight of the evening.

It made me want her.

More than I already did.

When we got back to her apartment, I walked CeCe to the door. "I had a great time tonight, Mr. Black. The food was excellent, the play was outstanding and you, sir, are a very good dancer."

"I just stood near you and tried not to look bad."

"So," CeCe said when we got to her door. "Do you know what it was that I wanted tonight?"

"Was it something other than dinner and dancing?"

"Yes."

"What was that?"

"I wanted something most people don't get. I wanted a second chance."

"Second chance at what?"

"A second chance at making a first impression." CeCe unlocked the door, but didn't open it. "You had the wrong impression of me, Mr. Black. I had to show you that I wasn't the woman you thought I was. I had to introduce you to the real me."

"You didn't have to go through all that," I said, but I was glad that she did. I saw CeCe in a completely different light now.

"Yes, I did. If I didn't, you would have never gotten to know me. You might have gotten around to having sex with me. But you would've never invited me out for an evening like the one we just had."

"I might have."

"No you wouldn't, because you didn't see me that way. You saw me as a soldier, a pawn on your chessboard. A knight at best, 'cause I get things done for you."

"I hate to admit it, but you're right. Right about a lot of things you've said about me."

"This is a good thing, at least I hope so anyway." CeCe opened the door. "Well, goodnight, Mr. Black. I'd invite you in, but I don't want you to think that I was the type of woman who has sex on the first date."

I looked at her like she was stupid, but if that's the way she wanted to play it, it was all good. I was just glad that I didn't send Kevon home.

"Good night, CeCe."

CeCe leaned forward, took my hand, and kissed me on the cheek. She leaned back, but didn't let go of my hand when I started to walk away.

Instead, she pulled me back gently and kissed me again, on the lips this time; and began backing her way into her apartment.

CeCe reached behind her back and attempted to unzip her dress. Since she was still walking backwards she was having problems, so I pulled her to my chest. CeCe loosened my tie and unbuttoned my shirt. I unzipped her dress and let it fall to the floor. I unhooked her bra and slid it off her shoulders. CeCe kicked out of her shoes and undid my pants.

When were naked, CeCe took me by the hand and led me to her room. She lay down in bed next to me and ran my hand across her breasts. I teased them with my tongue, sliding it slowly around her beautiful, dark circles. When CeCe spread her legs, I fingered her clit and CeCe moaned. CeCe kissed me passionately, and I reached out for CeCe and gently moved her body so I could taste her. I ran my tongue along her lips and proceeded to lick her clit. She moaned with pleasure.

CeCe repositioned herself and got on top of me. I looked on as she lowered herself onto me slowly. While she took me into the wetness between her thighs, CeCe stared into my eyes. "I have wanted this for so long."

I lay on my back and watched her move. Each movement was agonizingly slow and deliberate. I felt her body quiver. "Ooooh!" she cried.

CeCe rolled off of me and I watched her crawl around on the bed. Her ass was perfection. I ran my hands along her back, around her perfect ass then squeezed her firm thighs. I got up on my knees and entered her from behind. I felt the muscles inside her tighten around me. Her pussy was so soft, so wet, and I knew that I was absolutely right about her.

CeCe was a very dangerous woman.

One that I could have avoided.

But that's a story for another day.

Chapter 39

Nine months and twenty-three days later

Things have been good lately. Much better than I expected actually.

Martin Marshall won his election as congressman for his district. I used the check that Travis brought back from the Caymans for Martin's campaign. It paid for a few dirty tricks he said he needed money for, and as the election got closer, I put some money in the street which boosted voter turnout. Since then, Martin has proven to be a very valuable ally.

Shortly after J.R. came home to recover from his heart attack, he had a stroke that left him paralyzed on the right side of his body, and his speech badly impaired. With J.R. incapacitated, her brother in jail and Jeff Ritchie dead, Rain turned to Nick. In exchange for my help with her brother's case, Rain handed Nick J.R.'s gambling operations on a silver platter.

Wanda recommended that Miles plead not guilty of the murder due to temporary insanity, and wave his right to a jury trial. The prosecution thought they had a slam duck until I got his case heard in front of a sympathetic judge. A judge Martin gave me.

Under oath, each witness testified that they saw Miles and Jeff Ritchie fighting, and then Miles shot him. Thanks to Nick, none of the witnesses could remember seeing Miles leave and come back with the gun. The judge concluded that, after hearing that Jeff Ritchie had arranged the murder of the mother of his child, that Miles's mental condition at the time of the killing rendered the him unable to determine right from wrong, or that what he was doing was wrong. The Judge ordered clinical treatment until Miles could be certified safe to be released back into the community.

However, things haven't gone all that well for DEA agent Pete Vinnelli. Once the article hit the newsstands he was placed on administrative leave pending investigation. The Justice Department moved very quickly to freeze his assets, including the offshore accounts that were in the name of Eileen McManus.

After receiving the picture of Vinnelli and Pamela Connote, Eileen McManus went after Vinnelli with a gun. Emptying the clip on him. But since she wasn't a good shot, she only hit him once in the shoulder. She was arrested for attempted murder and money laundering. In exchange for consideration on the money laundering charge, McManus agreed to testify against Vinnelli. She pled guilty to aggravated assault and got five years.

With McManus in place, the DEA fired Vinnelli and he was indicted for money laundering and conspiracy to commit murder. That afternoon, Vinnelli fled the country for Nogales, Mexico.

Why do they always run to Mexico?

Nogales is one of many Mexican towns on the border with the United States. If you follow Interstate 19 south of Tucson, Arizona, you'll end right at the border from Nogales, Arizona to Nogales, Sonora, Mexico.

Monika and I drove down 19 and took the International Border exit. In no time at all, we saw the signs for parking lots on the American side. "You think the car will be safe here until we get back?" Monika wanted to know. She had become my secret weapon. Monika handles all the little things that Freeze used to do for me and so much more.

A man assured us that the car and its contents would be safe. We paid the fee and headed toward the border. What I noticed as I approached the border was the absence of armed troops. Across the street there were a few men in white shirts. "U.S. Border Patrol," Monika said.

Apparently, it was a busy shopping day with people crossing from Nogales into the U.S. to stock up on supplies. Women with baby strollers were returning back into Mexico with their purchases and joined us at the border turnstiles. Walking into Mexico was simple. No one even asked for our identification.

No one even eyed us.

After spending the day in a little dump of a bar, trading shots of tequila with Monika, Vinnelli finally showed up. It was obvious to both of us that he had been drinking heavily. "You sure about this?" I asked.

"You worry too much. I can handle him, now go on and get out of here."

"See you later." I finished my drink and stood up. Took a look at our prey and left Monika to do her work. I went back to our dump of a hotel, put my silencer on my gun, got a bottle of tequila, took a seat by the window and waited for Monika to get there.

It was an hour later when I heard noises in the hallway. I picked up my gun and pointed it at the door. Monika opened the door and in walked Vinnelli.

"Oh shit," he said when he saw me sitting there and the gun pointed at him.

He thought about leaving, but Monika put the gun to his head. "Get in there," she said and pushed him to the ground. Monika closed the door and stood over Vinnelli, putting the silencer on her gun. When she was ready I got up and walked to the spot where Vinnelli was on his knees with his hands in the air.

I thought about the monologue that I was gonna say before I killed him, about how foolish it was to fuck with me and shit like that. But now, here at the end, I felt nothing like I thought I would. I felt no anger, no pain, none of the rage that has consumed me since the night I came home and found Cassandra dead.

I looked at Vinnelli. He was a broken man. I had taken everything from him and turned him into a drunk. I began to feel sorry for him.

I lowered my gun.

Monika wasn't feeling sympathetic. Her first shot was aimed at his dick. "That's for callin' me a nigga bitch and still thinkin' you were gettin' some of this pussy."

I laughed while Vinnelli screamed.

Her second shot was aimed at his hand. "That's for touching me."

Vinnelli let out another loud scream and Monika stepped up and put the gun to his head.

"Any last words?"

"Finish it," Vinnelli said quietly and shed a tear.

Monika stepped back and I raised my gun again.

Both of us fired.

"Rest in peace, Cassandra."

I want to take this opportunity to thank everyone
that has read what I've written and supported me
over the years.

I love you all.

I have to go now.

I don't know when I'll return.

Good-bye. . . .